THE VANISHING HOLES MURDERS

Dexter Hadley hired Mark Preston to investigate his wife's behavior, but was murdered before Preston could begin. Hadley's employers then wanted Preston to look into some shenanigans at their tractor plant. A client claimed that a model had been delivered with a number of holes drilled into the bodywork, but when the machine was returned, the holes had disappeared. Soon, Preston found himself facing more tangible problems — like men with guns, and the irascible Rourke of Homicide.

PETER CHAMBERS

THE VANISHING HOLES MURDERS

Complete and Unabridged

LINFORD
Leicester

First published in Great Britain

First Linford Edition
published 1996

British Library CIP Data

Chambers, Peter, *1924* –
The vanishing holes murders.—Large print ed.—
Linford mystery library
1. English fiction—20th century
2. Large type books
I. Title
823.9'14 [F]

ISBN 0–7089–7942–4

Published by
F. A. Thorpe (Publishing) Ltd.
Anstey, Leicestershire
Set by Words & Graphics Ltd.
Anstey, Leicestershire
Printed and bound in Great Britain by
T. J. Press (Padstow) Ltd., Padstow, Cornwall

This book is printed on acid-free paper

1

THREE thousand, six hundred and forty two dollars.

I spread it out lovingly on the desk and stared at it. A genuine, one hundred per cent three-horse parlay, and it was mine, all mine. It isn't every day a man even picks one winner. To get three in a row that way is against all kinds of odds, and I'd done it. There probably isn't anyone who doesn't know what a three-horse parley is, but just in case Rip Van Winkle has just woken up, I'd better explain.

You see Rip, what it is, you examine the list of runners in a horse-race, and you decide which one is going to win. Then you bet on him. If he beats the rest to the post, you collect. That's an ordinary wager. But, with a parlay, you leave the money to ride. You have a horse in the next race, which you also

1

think is going to win. All the money from the first horse now goes on to this second horse, and he had better win, because if he doesn't, you collect dollars nil. Hooray for our side, he does win, but you still don't pick up the cash, because you have yet another nag in the next race, and the whole pot rides on his nose. You begin to develop doubts about this horse, who no longer seems as promising as he did before you bet all that money on him. In fact, now that you examine him closely, he looks a little splay-footed, and he sweats too much. Besides, you've never really trusted that particular jockey, who's already been the subject of official enquiries twice in the past year. By the time the flag goes up, you realise what a terrible mistake you have made, putting all that green stuff in the hands of such an obvious crook. Even if he tries to win, what chance does he have on that sway-backed gluepot you've chosen? He confirms all this by starting out seventh in a field of seven, and you are now in need of medical supervision. A great roar goes up, and you stare at the frame out of idle curiosity, wondering which of the other horses you should have selected. What have we here? There is your number, up in the top slot, and you have won. Three times in a row, and that is a three-horse parlay. There are two races left to run, and you have the name of a sure thing in each one. With all that money, this is your chance to clean out the track. But, take my advice Rip, and do what I did. Pick up the money and run all the way home. Leave the sure things to other experts, because there is only one golden rule. Always quit while you're ahead.

I was ahead. Three thousand, six hundred — or did I already mention that? A sound in the outer office warned me that Florence Digby had returned from her errand, and I set about scooping up the bills. Florence is officially my confidential secretary and personal assistant, at least that's what I tell people. It's good for my image, and gives me a proper standing, status-wise, in the world of business. Unofficially, she runs the whole operation, except for minor areas, such as detective work and bruise-collecting. When it comes to reports, records, correspondence and all that hooha, she is the one who presses the button, even to the paying of bills. Especially the paying of bills. Florence never seems quite to grasp our splendid financial system of ninety-day credits, pay nothing now, and yours on thirty-day free inspection. Where she comes from, bills are documents of shame, to be paid at once, receipted and filed away. If she caught sight of all that money, she would steal it from me, and rush around paying this, that and the other.

The quick tap at the door, and the sudden turning of the handle told me I was too late. Half the money was in my fist, an untidy spread of twenties and fifties, the rest was still in plain sight.

"Well, well."

Nobody can say 'well, well' quite like Florence. She is a lady of a certain age, and handsome in a forbidding kind of way, always immaculately turned out, and cool as a cucumber, no matter what the shade-temperature is outside. And there she stood, taking in the scene, with that well-well expression on her face. I decided to brave it out.

"I was lucky out at Palmtrees today," I said breezily.

"So I see," she returned evenly. "How much did you win?"

"I was just going to count it," I assured her. "Must be close to a thousand dollars, I fancy."

"There are twelve hundred and sixty dollars on the desk," she informed me, "and that doesn't include what you're trying to hide in your hand."

Women are supposed to be inept at figure-work. It doesn't seem fair that I should be stuck with a walking computer.

"Really? Well, I was just thinking, maybe I should get down to the bank."

"Better give it to me, Mr Preston," she countered. "I shall be doing the monthly summary tomorrow. This could change the picture in our favor, I trust."

I nodded miserably as she began to gather up my hard-earned winnings, and surrendered the stuff in my hand.

"A thousand dollars, indeed," she scoffed, "there's over three thousand here."

"I'll need a couple of hundred of that," I said quickly. "Have to pick up a few things. Better make that three hundred."

She hesitated, then put the bills in front of me with obvious reluctance.

"There's a visitor outside," she announced. "We walked in together. A man named Hadley."

I didn't want a visitor named Hadley. I wanted to sit and brood on the unfairness of life in general, and Florence Digby in particular.

"What's he like?" I asked, hoping to find some excuse for turning him away.

"Wasp," she pronounced. "Socio-economic group B1 at least. You ought to see him."

Other people might have said the man outside was well-dressed, or tall, dark and handsome, or something a listener could understand. If I wanted to know what he looked like, I was going to have to see him for myself.

"Well," I shrugged, "we mustn't keep a B1 Wasp waiting, must we?"

Sweeping up the last of my money, she went out, leaving the door ajar.

"Please come in Mr Hadley," she cooed.

He was five feet eight or nine, and too heavy at a hundred and eighty pounds, inside a gray business suit which was hand-tailored. The round baby face was ornamented by a pair of gold rimmed half-glasses, and the fair wavy hair on his head was beginning to thin. He'd had the whole presentation for thirty odd years.

"Mr Preston?" he asked, in a clipped voice, "I am Dexter Hadley."

I stood up to shake the pudgy, manicured hand, and got a whiff of expensive after-shave, plus alcohol undertones.

"Won't you sit down Mr Hadley. What can I do for you?"

He parked carefully, smoothing out the suit, composing the crease in his pants. Mr Hadley was a neat man.

"I must say," he opened, "this isn't quite what I expected."

'This', as indicated by a wave of his hand, included the whole layout, and probably me with it. It was not the first time I'd had the experience, and I nodded resignedly.

"You mean there ought to be a pint of whisky on the desk, and a raincoat tossed in one corner? I'm used to it, Mr Hadley. The Brothers Warner have a lot to answer for."

"The Brothers — ?" he began, looking mystified, then registering the point. "Ah, Warner Brothers, the movie people. Yes, yes, I see what you mean. Very good."

As if to demonstrate that he knew a joke when he heard one, he parted the tight lips one-eighth of an inch. Not quite far enough to confirm that there were any teeth behind them. Then he became almost expansive.

"You see, I am not accustomed to — that is to say, this is my first experience of — um — "

" — someone like me," I finished for him. "Don't worry about it, Mr Hadley. Ninety per cent of my clients are seeing someone like me for the first time in their lives. It's usually the only time, you'll be glad to hear."

I looked at him encouragingly. Sometimes they come right out with it. Other times we have to strike up an acquaintance, via the weather, the sorry condition of the stock market, and the baseball scores.

"It's about my wife," he said, right off the bat.

Good. I sat back, trying to look reliable.

"What's her name, Mr Hadley?"

"Rosanna. Well," he amended, "it's Joyce really, but she won't use that. Her middle name is Rosanna, and that's what she likes to be called."

I couldn't see the objection, but people can be odd about their names. Perhaps Call-me-Rosanna Hadley felt there was more romance in her middle name. A distant whisper of the bull-ring, the masked intruder, steamy Mediterranean goings-on. It would be a small rejection of her socio-economic B1 spouse, and their predictable years ahead.

"And how long have you been married?" I asked.

"Why do you want to know that?"

He seemed oddly defensive, as though I was prying unnecessarily.

"I don't, really," I shrugged. "It's just that some people like me to keep the conversation going. Put them at their ease, you might say."

"Oh. Yes, I can see that. Four years, as a matter of fact. That could be one of the problems. Rosanna is thirty-one, you see. She'd probably kill me if she knew I told you that."

The last remark wasn't to be taken literally. It's one of those things people say from time to time, without thinking. In my world, the word is used sparingly, and has to be used very carefully indeed.

"I've already forgotten it," I assured him. "But what makes it important?"

He spread the well-kept hands.

"No family," he explained. "We're both perfectly healthy people, and there's no medical reason that we can trace, but it just doesn't happen."

"I've heard of that before. It isn't uncommon. People sometimes go along for years, and then all of a sudden, there you are."

"I know," he agreed. "That's what I keep telling myself. Anyway, as I say, that could be part of it. My wife has been acting oddly these past

11

months. Goes missing from the house without explanation. Once or twice I've interrupted her while she's on the telephone, and she cuts off with some obvious platitude. I'm beginning to think that maybe there's someone else."

One of those. It began to sound as though my visitor had come to the wrong address.

"My Hadley, before you go on, I think I ought to tell you that I don't undertake divorce work. There are several good firms in town, and I can give you the names if you wish — "

"Divorce? Who said anything about divorce?" He sounded shocked.

"It's just that the general run of what you are telling me seems to point in that direction," I explained lamely.

"The general run of what I am telling you," he corrected, "is intended to indicate that I am very concerned about my marriage, and I want to do all I can to put it right."

My prospective client did not care for people jumping to conclusions. He was in the business of laying out the facts in his own good time, and others were not expected to make premature assumptions.

"I shouldn't have interrupted," I acknowledged. "What is it you want me to do?"

He fiddled with his tie, which was already perfectly correct. He didn't really want to listen to himself saying the next part.

"I want to know what she's up to. Where she goes, who she sees. After all, it could all be something quite innocent."

The last few words were uttered in a tone almost of challenge, as though we were arguing about it. I stared back at him.

"It could indeed," I agreed. "On the other hand, it might not. I might come up with things you don't want to hear. Are you sure you really want to hire me, Mr Hadley? Wouldn't it be better to have some kind of confrontation with your wife? After all, if you're not looking for a divorce, why involve a stranger?"

For a moment, he was silent. When he spoke again, it was in the subdued tones of a man who didn't like to talk about himself.

"Because I'm afraid," he admitted. "I feel that if I force the issue, I may drive Rosanna into some corner. She might even walk out on me, and that's the last thing I want. This way, I can arm myself with solid facts, and make a reasoned plan as to how to deal with the situation, whatever it is. It's the way I'm made, the way I've been trained, and it helps me avoid mistakes."

That I could believe. He had organisation-man stamped all over him, and he wasn't in the business of rushed decisions. What he would do, when he found out about the bullfights was anybody's guess. I didn't especially want the job, but the fees would be useful. If Florence Digby had been five minutes later in getting back to the office, I would still have had my winnings, and I could have shown Hadley the door. As things stood, I needed the assignment.

"I'm expensive, Mr Hadley. Three hundred a day, plus expenses. How long do you want me to stay with this?"

He seemed relieved, not that the decision was taken from him.

"As long as it takes," he replied. "Money is the least of my problems."

Nice for some.

"All right," I pulled a notepad towards me and pulled out my silver pencil. "I'd better have your home address, and your phone number. Also, a number where I can reach you during the day."

"I've brought my card. Here."

He slid the white card across the desk. The Hadleys lived at Oak Valley, an expensive area on the desert side of town. My new client was a C.P.A. which came as no surprise.

"Thank you. And the daytime number?"

"I can't give you that," he refused. "All calls come through the switchboard, and I daren't take any risk of anyone finding out what I'm doing."

I made a face.

"Mr Hadley, if I have anything to report, I can scarcely call you at home," I pointed out. "With your wife listening, you'll be talking in monosyllables and we'll never get anywhere."

"That's true," he admitted. "Very well, I'll make a point of calling you, here at the office, each afternoon. That way, we can keep in touch."

It was the best I was going to get.

"Very well. One last thing, I'll need a photograph of your wife. Did you bring one?"

He looked surprised.

"Why, no. I didn't think of it."

And him a C.P.A.

"I'm afraid I can't operate without one," I said gently. "Any woman coming out of No. 2223 could be

Mrs Hadley for all I know. Don't forget, I can hardly bang on the door of your apartment and introduce myself."

"Yes, of course, it was foolish of me. I'll have one here for you first thing tomorrow. Is there anything else you need?"

"Does she have her own car? If so, it would help me to know the make and license plate number."

He gave me the information, and I wrote it down. Then I nodded.

"That's about it, Mr Hadley. As soon as I have that picture, I'll go to work. Shall we say I start booking my time from tomorrow morning?"

"Yes. I'd like you to get started right away. I thought this would be a satisfactory retainer."

'This' was a thin spread of bills, five in all, and each marked at one hundred dollars. It seemed to be raining money today.

"Cash, Mr Hadley?" I queried.

"I prefer it, I shall settle with you in cash too. No cheques. I want our business to remain entirely between the two of us."

"As you wish," I gathered in the harvest. "I guess that's about it, then."

He got to his feet, evidently relieved that the session was ended.

"That will be satisfactory, Mr Preston. And I will call you tomorrow afternoon."

I didn't think there would be any point. The chances of my having learned anything in one morning were infinitesimal, but I didn't tell him that. Instead, I looked encouraging, and nodded.

"Fine."

He went away then, and Florence Digby replaced him within seconds of the door closing.

"Our new client is a C.P.A." I informed her.

She nodded importantly, having expected nothing less.

"Shall I open a file?"

"Start booking my time as of tomorrow morning," I handed her the business card. "Let me have that back when you're through. This is a tail job on Mrs Hadley."

It's always a pleasure to surprise La Digby.

"Divorce?" she queried. "That's unusual. We're not that hard-pressed."

"No it is not divorce," I contradicted nastily, "it is a tail job, and that's all. Oh, and I may need Thompson, if he's conscious. Put out the feelers, see if you can locate him."

At the mention of the name, her face became more haughty than usual, and she went away. An outsider would have jumped to the understandable conclusion that Miss Digby did not approve of Sam Thompson, and an outsider would be wrong. He is a great shambling figure of a man who is really quite capable of making something of himself, and he would do it, too, but for the effort involved. Effort is a department in which Thompson does not shine. His idea of a strenuous day is to hoist himself up on a barstool and remain there until the money runs out. So long as the financial position remains liquid, Thompson stays ditto, but the economic principle always applies in the end. No work, no drink. At these times, he can be persuaded to undertake certain forms of paid activity, and one of these is to act as leg-man for me. He is one of the best in the business, and could have had his own agency long since but for his deep-rooted antipathy to all forms of activity. He probably thinks of himself as the last of the free spirits, but most people would think of a less charitable category. Especially people who use phrases like 'socioeconomic groups', which includes Florence Digby. Yet the Digby, for all her hoity-toity attitudes, has a soft spot for Thompson. The pillar of rectitude, with her clear-cut and predictable views on every other subject under the sun, develops cloudy thinking on the subject of the walking disaster area known as Sam Thompson Esquire. It's like someone said, 'show me the man who understands women, and I'll show you an idiot.'

I put the pair of them out of my mind, and wondered about Joyce, who shall be called Rosanna, Hadley. Without a photograph to guide me, I tried to build up a mental image of her, standing beside the precise Dexter Hadley, C.P.A. She would be short, for one thing. Hadley wasn't the type to have to spend all his days looking up at a female. Dark-haired, probably, on the principle of opposites. Well turned-out, because he would not permit otherwise, and discontented, by the sound of things. She would probably be on the fluffy side. Prim, stern characters like Hadley frequently elect for fluffy females, preferably not too bright so as to present no challenge to their authority. Yes, I had a pretty good idea of what to expect. After all, I haven't been in the detective business all these years without picking up a few wrinkles.

Well, she would have to wait until tomorrow. For the moment, I had three hundred dollars in my pocket, narrowly rescued from the grasping fingers of my so-called assistant. It was less than ten per cent of the day's take, but nonetheless sufficient to cover an evening on the town. I also had a further five Cs, to tuck away against a rainy day. All this sleuthing work can exhaust a man, and a little relaxation would seem in order. I sat around for a while, turning over a few possibilities in my mind, then I called it a day and went home.

Home is a four-roomed apartment in Parkside Towers, up at the Heights. It's an expensive address, and the outgoings are murderous, but I'd been the fleabag route in my early years, and Parkside is better. The way I see it, a man owes it to himself to take a little comfort while he can. Some people take it in the shape of fluffy items named Rosanna, but I'll hang on to my independence for just a little while longer.

There were a couple of items of junk mail in the box, and I read as much as

I could, between the front door and the trash can in the kitchen. There was a half pot of coffee still standing from the morning, so I switched it on to re-heat and set about taking off my day-clothes. The early evening news was a repetition of the previous evening, the previous week, the previous year. A lot of gunfire in far-off places, rubble strewn streets and haunted faces. Leaders talking about peace, unwarranted aggression, armed intervention, non-intervention. Lots of maps with lines on them, and unpronounceable place-names. Worried men with brief-cases disappearing into the Pentagon while sardonic policemen kept a wary eye on a line of banner-wavers. Repetition dulls the senses, and the staccato, urgent delivery of the news-presenter had a soporific effect, quite the reverse of the dramatic impact intended. But for the date on the calendar, it could have been a re-run from last year, or five years ago. The local news was no better. Mayor Scroggs said that inner-city relief was now the number one priority. Councilman Boggs said that inflation was now positively on a downturn. Senator Coggs assured us that state taxes were now receiving attention at the highest level, while the only light relief of the day was left as always to Good-Causes Snoggs. He announced the formation of the Stray Dogs Relief Society, with immediate capitalisation of one million dollars, and two movie stars on the board of directors. Last week, it had been the American Language Reform Group. They only got one movie star that time, which possibly stresses the importance of the stray dogs in our daily lives.

At nine o'clock that evening, everything seemed set fair. I was at Alberto's, nursing a tall scotch over ice, and pacing myself carefully on the intake. It was important I should have a clear head at ten, because Mike Blair had promised to look in around then, for drinks and whatever. Mike is features editor on the Monkton City Globe, and as choice a female decoration as this city has on offer. She is also an extremely high-powered lady in the newspaper business, and nothing will tempt her away from the Globe offices until the last edition of the next day's issue has been put to bed. So there I was, decidedly mellow, and listening to the melodic improvisations of the fat man at the piano. It was a remarkable physical achievement, the way he could coax those intricate runs from fingers the size of sausages, and the delicacy of his touch seemed somehow incongruous, originating as it did from such a shapeless hulk.

The place was half-full, and all around was the subdued chatter, the comings and goings of unobtrusive waiters, and the general ambience of a place where people came for quiet enjoyment. That's what Alberto aims for, and that is what he gets. Any of the Hooray Charlie brigade get short shrift in that place. Among its other attractions, it features the quietest heave-ho squad in the business, and noisy customers sometimes find themselves back out on the street without knowing quite how they got there. People are not expected to raise their voices, and the man who now spoke over my shoulder evidently knew the rules.

"This is the life, huh Preston?"

I turned, at the familiar tones, to see my old friend Sergeant Gil Randall of Homicide, beaming at me. Randall is a man I prefer to see beaming. A great shambling ox of a man, he parades around with the kind of animation normally associated with the sloth, peering at the world from heavy-lidded eyes which are clearly one degree away from unconsciousness. Anyone who knows anything about people can tell at a glance that Randall is not too bright, and woefully unfit. You can see he's the type who has a mental struggle each day, remembering which shoe goes on which foot. That's the way people see him, and the jails are full of such people, still wondering how it all came about. I've known him too long to be suckered by that act of his. His mind would make a fair substitute for the average computer, complete with memory banks. As for his build, I've seen him move with the speed and precision of a ballet dancer against a gun or a knife, and he doesn't fool me one bit.

"Hallo Gil, I didn't know this was one of your haunts. Let me get you a drink."

"It isn't," he grunted, staring around. "No honest policeman can afford places like this. No honest anybody can. Still, if you're paying, I'll take a beer. It'll fill in the time while you're finishing that."

I waved at the barkeep. If Randall was accepting a drink, things weren't too bad. But there was no avoiding the import of what he said.

"Finishing this?" I queried. "Are we going somewhere?"

"Yup. Rourke wants to see you."

The beer glass disappeared into a hand like a side of bacon, and he tipped half the contents down his throat in one gulp.

"What does he want?" I asked.

Randall looked at me pityingly.

"You know how he is," he hedged. "Never tells me anything. 'Get Preston down here,' he said. That's all. I tell you it's like belonging to a secret society."

A likely story. They were as thick as thieves, those two, the sleepy giant Randall, and the dapper rattlesnake known as Lieutenant John Rourke. The most formidable combination in the state, as one newscaster once described them. I don't know about the others, but these two are quite enough for me. Another citizen might have made a protest, making noises about this being a free country, and we'll see what my congressman has to say about this, but other citizens don't have my problems. I have to live with these people, and I carry a little piece of identification which authorises me to pursue my calling as a private investigator. Said authority is subject to renewal, and renewal always entails a happy nod from the police department. Sure, it's a free country, and I could tell Randall to peddle his papers, but if I don't help them, why should they help me when the time comes? I wasn't very happy about standing up Miss Blair. She's not a lady who relishes that kind of treatment, and it would be a long time before she forgot and forgave.

Alberto watched my impending departure with anxiety. I shrugged, in an attempt to let him know this wasn't my idea.

"Miss Blair ought to get here soon," I said to him. "Could you tell her I got called away? I ought to be back here inside an hour."

I looked hopefully at Randall, but he did some shrugging of his own.

"Hard to tell," he evaded. "This man we have to see, you know the way he is. A chatterbox. Yakkity yak — you know."

Alberto didn't like it, but he contrived a small half-bow.

"I shall do my best with the lady," he confirmed.

Which was what I had hoped to be doing.

When I first arrived at the place, the evening had seemed warm and balmy, full of that West Coast promise. Leaving, I found there was a decided nip in the air.

2

THE headquarters of the Monkton City P.D. used to be the pride of the coast. It had the most up-to-date facilities for the peace officers, with comfortable rest rooms, and fine dry stabling for their horses. The citizens were justly proud of their efforts on behalf of the men with the tin stars, and turned their attention to other matters. The town grew, and so did the crime rate. Every few years, the administration would give its grudging consent to the expenditure of a few dollars to extend the accommodation of the police department, and there gradually evolved a random collection of temporary huts, additional stories and outbuildings. The resultant sprawl was now inadequate, insanitary and unsightly. Any attempt to employ such a place as a rest-home for war refugees, or even as a penal institution, would have brought howls of protest from every do-good organisation in the land. However, since it was only for the use of the city's law enforcement, which already cost enough, heaven knows, the complex was left as it was.

The Homicide Bureau occupies just three rooms on an upper floor. For the unwary, an aged wheezing elevator lurks at ground level, anxious to get about its business of trapping people between floors, but there are few takers. Regular customers, a description which sadly includes me, head straight for the worn and creaking stairway, with its flyblown decor and titillating graffiti. Randall and I plodded upward, reserving our breath for the effort, until we were outside the dirty half-glass door which read Homicide Bureau-J. Rourke, Captain of Detectives. That was another little saving on the city purse. Years before, when Rourke had first been given the job, he was already a full lieutenant. It was at a time of zero public expenditure, and he quite understood that although he would hold the rank and title of captain, it would not be possible to pay him the rate for the job until things eased off. As time passed, his understanding became less, but the situation remained the same, and the subject was no longer raised.

Rourke is physically not very big, but you can feel power radiating from him. A bundle of nervous energy and unpredictable temperament, and looks and acts like just what he is. A dynamic, incorruptible servant of the public, with reserves of strength in no way diminished by the advancing years.

He sat now behind his desk, in the small room he shared with Randall, looking up at our entrance, and nodding.

"Did he confess?"

He spoke directly to Randall, looking through me. The trouble with these two is, you never know when they're just kidding.

"Not yet," denied Randall. "He's

still pretending he doesn't know why he's here. I'll say one thing for him, he didn't give me any trouble."

"Ha ha," I grunted, looking around for a safe chair, and squatting on it. "What's this all about, John?"

He stared at me from piercing eyes.

"Well now," he said slowly, "let's take it in stages. You saw the sign on the door? It says 'Homicide'. That means we deal with all kinds of sudden death by unlawful means. That's what we do here. We don't deal with parking offenses or kids stealing apples, stuff like that. Murder, that's our dodge. Is it getting clearer?"

I wasn't in any mood for banter. At any minute, Mike Blair would be arriving at Alberto's and that was where I ought to be. Not sitting around gabbing it up with these characters.

"So somebody got bumped off. What's that to do with me?"

"Oh, not just somebody. Somebody very special, a dear close friend of yours. If you'd just tell us why you did it, we can all get a good nights sleep."

I looked up at Randall, who leaned against the wall, beaming encouragement.

"Who's the somebody?" I demanded.

Rourke looked pained.

"Don't you remember?" he queried.

"I kill a lot of people," I said nastily. "You can't expect me to carry all the details in my head."

He picked up a blue report sheet from the desk, and studied it.

"At eight seventeen this evening, Officers Gilbert and Larsen discovered the body of a man on waste ground off River Street. Man identified as Dexter Hadley, with an address in Oak Valley. He had been badly beaten, then killed by gunshots, seven in all. In his pocket was a piece of paper bearing the name of Mark Preston, and an address I think you would recognise. We certainly do. So, it will save us all the time and trouble if you fill in the details."

He sat back, waiting. For once, I

didn't have to construct some elaborate story, and I was grateful for that. My dealings with Hadley were all out in plain view, and with luck I'd be gone in ten minutes. I wondered briefly who killed him, but it was nothing to do with me.

"I only ever saw Hadley once, and that was today. He came to the office, and we talked for fifteen, twenty minutes. Then he went away, and that's all there is. So, if there's nothing further — "

I made a pretence of getting up, but Randall waved me back down with a disappointed finger.

"Such modesty," he reproved. "You're assuming we wouldn't be interested in your little conversation with the deceased. You're wrong. We want to know everything that was said. Everything."

I shrugged.

"Just routine. Hadley has — had — this wife, you see. Name of Joyce, but she likes to be called Rosanna.

Anyway, he got hold of my name, and — "

I went into the story, being careful to leave out nothing. Habit being the creature it is, I still found myself examining every morsel of information for possible traps before releasing it. It was completely pointless, since I had nothing to hide, but I'd been doing it so long it came automatically.

"And that's it?" asked a surprised Rourke.

"That's the whole thing," I assured him.

He nodded, smiling.

"Well, I think we have the picture now, don't you sergeant?"

"I think we do, captain," confirmed Randall.

"Yes, it's all quite clear I think. Preston here has been dallying with Mrs Hadley, and the husband found out. So Preston beat him up, shot him full of holes, and dumped him down on River Street."

"Looks that way," agreed Randall.

"Mrs Hadley probably helped him with the body, so we have them both. Shall I take him down?"

"In a little while. Just a few details to be cleared up.

I let them prattle on. Policemen, especially homicide experts develop a strange sense of humour, and I knew from experience they were kidding me. At the same time, I mustn't annoy them. If I did that they could keep me for the night as a material witness, and they'd done it before.

"You want me to play it again," I asked wearily.

"If you don't mind, Sam. It's one of my favorites."

We did it again, and I didn't make any of the little mistakes they were looking for, because there were none to be made. It gives a man a strange feeling of security to be telling the truth, the whole truth and etc etc. Finally, they grew tired of the game.

"So it wasn't you at all?" grumbled Rourke.

"Not this time. You'd do better with the boy friend," I suggested.

"Maybe," contributed Randall, "except we don't know who he is."

"Or if he is," added Rourke. "He'd be a strange kind of boy friend, toting all that artillery around."

"Plenty of people have guns," I suggested brightly.

They looked at each other as though arriving at a decision. Over the years they have developed a kind of telepathic shorthand of their own, and it's unsettling.

"As you say, plenty of people," agreed Randall. "But not many people have two guns, of different calibres, and use them both at the same time."

If Hadley had been killed in that fashion, it began to sound more like an execution than a murder.

"Are you saying the mob did this?" I asked. "Hadley was not exactly mob material. He probably considered a parking ticket a criminal record. Unless — "

"Unless what?" chimed Rourke quickly.

"Unless the boy friend was mixed up in the rackets," I suggested. "He could have had some of his people take care of the husband."

Rourke stared at the ceiling, and Randall expelled an exasperated breath.

"You watch too much television," he diagnosed. "This is the eighties, not the twenties. Those people only kill as a last resort these days. Your Mr Hadley wouldn't justify the hassle."

"What'll you do now, Preston?"

Rourke's question was unexpected, and I registered surprise.

"Do? About what?"

"Seems to me," he expounded, "you took money from this man, and you've done nothing for it. Maybe you should return it to the grieving widow. Five hundred, I think you said."

Between Florence Digby and these people, a man could wind up in a pauper's grave. I had an idea.

"I don't think that would be right," I

objected. "Here's this poor woman, her husband just murdered, and I turn up with all that money. Why did he give it to me? To check whether she was two-timing him. That's not a very nice last memory for her to keep, is it?"

"He has a point there, captain," said Randall. "But it still doesn't make it his money."

"You're right, sergeant. Mr Preston seems to have a problem."

The only problem Mr Preston had, seemed to be one of getting these two meddling humourists off his back. I looked from one impassive face to the other, trying to work out what was going on in their minds.

"How's this? Let's say there is a boy friend. You wouldn't know anything about that, because even Hadley wasn't sure, and that's why he hired me."

"Go on," invited Rourke.

"Well," I proceeded, "I feel kind of obligated to the late Hadley. How would it be if I just went ahead on that boy friend angle? Let's say I owe him two days. I could dig around, see if I turn up anything, then pass it over to you people. Least I can do."

Randall stared at Rourke, and Rourke stared at me. In disbelief.

"How would it be?" he echoed sourly. "It would be terrible, that's how it would be. If there is a boy friend, and if Mrs Hadley is mixed up in her husband's death, you can bet they'll stay well clear of each other this next few days. My officers will have to proceed with great care, if they're to learn anything. The last thing they want is to find somebody like you fouling up all the leads, and scaring everybody off. The last thing I want, is to have some fancy pants so-called investigator meddling in police business. Can you imagine what the newspeople would do with an idea like that? 'Worried police call in private help', that kind of stuff? We'd never live it down. Forget it."

I was very relieved to hear him say it. My proposal had really been aimed at steering their unwanted attention

42

away from my five hundred dollars and, hopefully, it had worked.

"Naturally," intoned Randall, "if anything comes your way which could throw any light on this little mystery, you'll pass it over to us. Just like any other citizen."

"Naturally," I agreed, but I didn't like the sound of it. It was almost as though Randall was telling me to go ahead and browse around, despite the hands-off notice I'd had from his boss.

"I'm sure we don't need to remind this fine upstanding citizen of his duty, sergeant," reproved the Irishman. "Why don't you take him away and get his statement, so that I can get on with some police work."

Randall motioned me out, and we went down to the empty squadroom to complete the formalities.

"What's up with you people?" I demanded. "Dragging me up here at this time of night, and scaring the hell out of me. This could have waited till morning."

Randall nodded imperturbably.

"Gives us a sense of power," he explained. "Besides, you're all we have. Mrs Hadley seems to be out for the evening, and there's no other family, so that only left us with you. What did you think of him?"

"Rourke? If I told you, you'd lock me up."

"Not Rourke," he corrected mildly, "your client, Hadley. What kind of a guy was he?"

"Average, I would say. Average to nondescript. He looked prosperous enough, but he didn't strike me as any world-beater."

"How about wife-beater?"

"That we'll never know."

"You're wrong about that," he rejected. "We'll know, and you can bet on it. And, speaking of betting, the word is you took Big Jule Keppler for ten grand today."

He looked at me enquiringly. It's always the same in this town. As soon as anybody shows a little profit at the track, or the tables, everybody starts to add zeros to the total. The bookies and the casino-owners do nothing to discourage the rumours. It's good for their business to have big winners in circulation, because it encourages everyone else to think they can do the same.

"Is that what the word is?" I scoffed. "Well, it's all pipe-talk. Three lousy grand, plus a few dollars, that was the score."

He nodded, half-expecting it.

"Still, a nice day's work," he offered. "What'll you do, take a few days off?"

"With what?" I demanded bitterly. "I don't have any money. Florence stole it from me. Something about bills, she said."

That seemed to cheer him up.

"Ah yes, Miss Digby. A very fine lady, that. How is she, these days?"

"Larcenous," I assured him. "You need somebody to lock up, the Digby is a straight forward case."

"Not my business," he returned

happily. "You need the Fraud people. Well now, let's get down to this murder you know nothing about."

It was after midnight when I made a not-too-hopeful return visit to Alberto's. The place was almost full this time, but noticeably deficient in lady feature-editors. I sat at the bar, and waited until the busy owner could find a moment for me.

"Ah, Mr Preston, the charming Miss Blair was here, but she couldn't wait," he explained, with regret.

"Did she leave any message for me?"

He shrugged.

"Not to say a real message," he denied, "but I have seen ladies, how shall I put it, in a better frame of mind."

It was no more than I expected, but it depressed me just the same. I finished my drink, and the hovering bartender looked at me enquiringly. A moment's hesitation, and I shook my head. Without Mike Blair, the evening was a bust.

"There's no point," I told him.

He was still trying to interpret that as I made my way back out into the night, and the lonely solace of Parkside Towers.

Next morning I was in the office before ten. Florence Digby nodded brightly as I went through. Let her enjoy her freedom, I thought darkly. I could have her locked up any time I liked. That's the kind of morning it was, and the kind of mood I was in. After a few moments, she followed me.

"I've managed to get in touch with Mr Thompson," she announced, "and he will telephone here at eleven this morning for instructions."

I'd forgotten all about him, with so much going on.

"I'm not going to need him after all," I informed her.

"But you said — " she began.

"I know what I said," I snapped, "but with the client dead, I don't have an assignment — "

Her hand went to her throat.

"Dead?" she repeated, startled. "You mean Mr Hadley? Whatever happened to him? I mean, he looked so well."

I had forgotten temporarily that Florence's idea of reading a newspaper consists of scanning the society column and the financial pages.

"He was murdered," I said. "Early last night. Therefore, I am unemployed. Therefore, Thompson is also unemployed. Now do you see?"

"Oh, my. Do they know who did it?"

"Not yet, but they will. You can't just go around bumping off B1 Wasps in this village and get away with it. Send Thompson twenty for his trouble, and explain the circumstances."

"Very well. Oh dear, I'm afraid I may have lost you an enquiry."

I stared at her, uncomprehending.

"Why? Did you knock off Mr Hadley?"

She clicked her teeth with impatience.

"Certainly not. How ridiculous. I'm talking about the call that came through this morning. A company wanted you to call, but I said you'd be all tied up for the next few days. I'm sorry, Mr Preston, but I had no idea."

For a moment, I was tempted to let it go, but then I reconsidered. The police had warned me off the Hadley thing, and a long day of thumb-twiddling stretched ahead.

"We all make mistakes," I conceded. "Try calling them back. I suppose they gave no indication of what they wanted?"

"No," she confirmed. "It was a woman who called. Personal Assistant to the Chairman of the company, so she said. The company is called Ag-Mach, and they manufacture agricultural machinery. The chairman is a Mr Morton Weill?"

She looked at me hopefully, to see if it rang any bells. I shook my head.

"Sorry. I don't do much farming these days."

"Well, I'll go and see if I can repair the damage."

A few minutes later she was back.

"I have Mr Weill's assistant on the line," she announced. "Mr Weill is now suggesting you call at the plant at eleven-thirty, if that fits in with your schedule."

"You want me to talk to her?"

"Quite unnecessary," she assured me, and her tone was frosty. "Miss Fordyce, that's her name, refused to contact Mr Weill. Said she handled such matters on his behalf."

The message was clear. Mr Weill was too important a person to deal with details. Evidently this Fordyce had tried to upstage Florence, and that's always a mistake. If Fordyce handled such matters for Weill, then Digby would do the same for Preston. I grinned.

"O.K. Florence, you go ahead and fix it up. I'll be there."

3

THE Ag-Mach company proved to be located in the area east of town known to the locals as Dust Valley. Some of the earlier settlers, having missed the regular route, had come to grief in that waterless, harsh area, with no way of knowing they were just a few miles from the promised land.

A twenty minute drive, these days, would have been a two-day haul then, and staring out at the shimmering, pitiless desolation, it was easy to imagine the despair it could cause. Finally, I reached a large wooden sign, announcing that I would have to make a left half a mile ahead, and it was cheering to have the assurance that somebody else besides me had survived the conditions.

I could see the plant now, a large

sprawl of buildings stuck in the middle of nowhere, and soon I was pulling up at the open entrance gates, where an elderly man emerged from a wooden shack, blinking at me from thick pebble glasses.

"Howdy," he greeted. "Who did you want to see?"

"Howdy," I replied, just to be in the spirit of the thing, "I'm calling on Mr Weill. Where do I go?"

"Boss man," he informed me importantly. "You'll find him in that tall white building over there. The one with the air-conditioning."

A sore point evidently. I was to infer there was no such amenity to be found in the wooden structure behind him. Thanking him, I drove to where he pointed, and parked outside. The old man was right, the temperature inside was many degrees cooler. A bright-faced kid sat at a combination reception-desk and telephone switchboard, and she looked at the newcomer with interest.

They probably didn't get too many of us prospectors calling in, but she knew how to handle it.

"My name is Preston," I told her. "I have an eleven-thirty appointment to see Mr Weill."

"Oh yes, Mr Preston," she cooed. "Won't you take a seat, please? There are magazines on the table."

That was what she'd been trained to say, and I didn't want to spoil it for her. I nodded my thanks, and went to sit in a white leather and steel contraption which I'd last seen in the background on Space Rangers 2000. The magazines had probably come from the same program, being concerned solely with technical developments in various fields. There were no pictures of Miss Earth Mover, and no agony columns to read.

"Mr Preston?"

I hadn't heard her approach, but I was glad she came. Tall, at least five eight, and rangy inside a yellow cotton dress, severely cut. Brown hair was layered flat to her head, and the long planes of her face ended in a decisive jaw line. The regular-shaped nose was a little too large and so was the mouth, now upturned at the corners in enquiry. In fact, there wasn't one feature that was perfect, but when you put all her imperfections together, you came up with only one overall result. Knockout.

I got quickly to my feet.

"Yes, I'm Preston," I confirmed. There wasn't much room for doubt, since the reception hall was otherwise deserted, but it was the best I could think of.

"I'm Margaret Fordyce, Mr Weill's personal assistant," she greeted. "If you will come with me, Mr Weill will see you directly."

I would go with her. To see Mr Weill, or to any other destination she cared to name. La Digby had sold this one short. I'd been left with an impression of some virago who would need to be put in her place, and

Margaret Fordyce came as something of a shock. Instead of being fifty, she was thirty, and the expected steel-rimmed spectacles would have looked incongrous over those luminous green eyes.

"This is quite a place," I said chattily. "It's an odd location for such a busy operation."

"It was built here quite deliberately during World War Two," she informed me. "It was a defense plant originally, so when this company was expanding a few years back, the whole package was available at a price which was only half what it would have cost in the city."

We were in the elevator now, and the interview with Weill was drawing closer, which meant my time with the guide-lady was equivalently lessening.

"Do you come out from Monkton every day?"

The doors slid open, and I waited for her to step out first. In the carpeted corridor, she looked at me thoughtfully.

"Why yes," she confirmed. "The

only other town within twenty miles is Rositer Springs, and nobody lives there under eighty years old. This is Mr Weill's office."

She tapped at the door, opening it, and putting the brown head round.

"Mr Preston for you."

Then she stood back, inclined her head at me, and I thanked her, walking inside. The door was pulled to behind me, and she was gone. I looked at Mr Weill, and he was no substitute. Medium height and nearly bald, he had the build of an all-in wrestler, brought down by soft living. The flabby features were shaved clean, with purple cheeks either side of an upturned, too-small nose. He looked at me from pale eyes which were recessed deeply in wrinkled pouches, and the whole effect was porcine. Yes, that was undoubtedly the word. Mr Weill looked like an extremely clean pig.

"Come on in Mr Preston, and take a seat." He remained seated, pointing to a chair, which was the twin of the one

I'd just vacated. "It's a hot drive, would you care for some iced lemonade?"

"Thank you, I could use that."

He didn't seem to do anything about it, but nodded his head as if satisfied.

"Very good you could come," he continued. "Mrs Fordyce said at first that you were all tied up."

I kept him waiting longer for an answer than I ought, but I was still hearing that 'Mrs'. Then I said.

"Yes, that was because my secretary didn't know at the time, I'd finished the work I was doing."

"Well, I'm glad it all worked out," he beamed. "Ah."

He broke off as the door opened and Margaret Fordyce came in with a tray. The pitcher of lemonade clanked with ice cubes, and there were two tall glasses. Setting the tray down, she poured out, and carried the glasses to us. As she handed mine over, there seemed to be a look in her eyes which could have been devilment. Or mockery. Or my imagination. I thanked her, and she set the other glass down carefully in front of her boss.

"Thank you Margaret."

We both waited until the door closed behind her. I took a drink of the cold, slightly bitter drink. So many people ruin it with too much sugar.

"I don't suppose you were completely surprised to hear from us?" asked Weill.

I hadn't the faintest idea of what he was talking about, and I must have looked as surprised as I felt.

"Well as a matter of fact, Mr Weill, it was a total surprise to me," I contradicted. "Matter of fact, I never heard of your company till today. This isn't exactly my line of work."

If he was surprised in turn, he managed to conceal it better.

"Oh. Well, then it looks as though I'm going to have to start at the beginning. It's about Dexter Hadley, you see. Are you telling me you didn't know he worked here?"

That cleared up one point but left

several others in its place.

Morton Weill had assumed that Hadley would have told me about his employment, which explained his opening remark. It did not explain how he knew that Hadley had been to see me, nor what made it any concern of Ag-Mach.

"No," I denied, "it didn't come up. Mr Hadley came to see me about a private matter. It has nothing to do with his business life."

"Ah," Weill seemed to be greatly committed to Ohs and Ahs. "Then I had better tell you that he was our Deputy Financial Administrator."

I nodded, and waited for more.

"His being killed that way has come as a terrible shock to us all," he went on. "And, quite frankly, it leaves us in a very embarrassing situation."

He seemed to be finding this part difficult, and I thought it might help if I made a contribution.

"You're going to have to explain that Mr Weill. As I said, Hadley told me nothing about his work. To tell you the truth, I probably wouldn't have understood if he'd tried. The workings of organisations like this are something of a mystery to me. Let me ask you a question. Dexter Hadley didn't strike me as the kind of man who would discuss his private affairs with anyone, not even his boss. How does it come about that you know he'd been to see me?"

"I should have thought that was obvious," he replied, on a rising tone. "The police told me. Dragged me out of bed last night, must have been close to twelve o'clock. It was a big man, Sergeant Rendall, I think — "

"Randall," I corrected.

"Randall, then. Wanted to know when I'd last seen Dexter, whether he had any financial problems, anything I knew about his private life. He also mentioned you. Was there anything I could think of, which would cause Dexter to approach someone like yourself. It was a very distressing experience I assure you. I didn't see why it couldn't have waited until the morning, and I told him so."

I could bet that he did, too. Weill was not a man to accept being pulled out of bed to answer a lot of police questioning, and I could visualise his reaction. At the same time, I could imagine the impassive Randall, unimpressed by Weill's importance, and grinding away with his interrogation. Comforting to have confirmation that all income-groups get the same treatment when there's a murder on the table.

"Randall would have had no choice, Mr Weill," I soothed. "In these cases, the police need every scrap of information as early as possible. Trails get cold, memories fade, and guilty people have more chance of building up alibis and so forth. It's a nuisance, but they have to do these things. They did the same to me, only worse. In my case they broke up an important social appointment. They even threatened to lock me up."

He had listened with interest, and now looked surprised.

"Lock you up? For what?"

"For being a man who was careless enough to have his name and address in the pocket of another man, who got himself killed. There's a nasty piece of legislation covering people called material witnesses. Gives them the right to slam the door on anybody, and on any old excuse."

"But they didn't do it?" he queried. "Arrest you, I mean?"

"No. It's a kind of game that we play. Sometimes they take me in, and sometimes they don't. Mostly, they do it to remind me who's who around this town."

"I see," he nodded doubtfully, like a man who didn't see at all.

"Anyway, that is what brings us together this morning. I am vitally interested in this terrible business, and it goes deeper than just being a good employer. Would you be willing to take on an assignment, Mr Preston?"

I stared at the floating cubes of ice, now shrinking from the warmth of my hand. This didn't sound good at all. It was only natural that Hadley's employers would want to do all they could to help out his widow, and stuff like that. The setting up of an investigation of their own was decidedly out of character, and I felt uneasy. At the same time I was curious, and wanted to know more before I turned it down.

"It would depend," I hedged. "Last night, the police were just making noises. I'm used to it, and we all know the rules. But if they thought I was seriously meddling in what is entirely a police matter, the position would alter, and to my detriment. What exactly is it that you have in mind, Mr Weill?"

The eyes retreated even further within their little pouches. Mr Weill was not a man who was accustomed to people putting up barriers. Mr Weill was a man who told you what to do, and you went out and did it.

"Before I get into that," he demurred, "I'd like to have our legal position regularised. As I understand it, you have a right under the law to maintain client-confidentiality?"

"To an extent," I agreed.

"Very well. Now, in order for you to decide whether to accept my commission, I am going to have to take you into my confidence. As I see it, an opening conversation like that would not bind you in any way, which is not acceptable. I propose to regard you as working for Ag-Mach for one day, in other words today. After that, if you don't wish to proceed, the matter ends. But," he emphasised heavily, "you would be ethically bound to reveal nothing of what I say. Is it agreed?"

I didn't need to think that one over. The man was offering to pay for my time, win or lose.

"Agreed."

Satisfied, he slid open a drawer,

and produced some bills, which he slid across to me.

"That includes fifty dollars for expenses."

My first impression of Mr Weill seemed to have been a little harsh. He was improving by the minute.

"We have a deal, Mr Weill. Suppose you tell me the story."

"I shall begin with Dexter Hadley," he opened. "As Deputy Financial Administrator he had a wide range of duties. People tend to over-simplify when they think of accountants. They have a vague notion of them as people who collect money and pay out money, and try to keep the books balanced. That, in fact, is no more than book-keeping, and almost anyone can do it. A real accountant does far more, and we should be here all day if we tried to cover the whole range. But it is necessary for me to elaborate just a little, so that you may have a clear picture."

I tried to look intelligent, but I

was hoping this conversation wouldn't become too technical. Elementary book-keeping gave me enough headaches, as it was.

"Hadley controlled the costing procedures, which involves a detailed analysis of all our processes. Everything, from the purchase of raw materials to the salary of the man who puts the final lick of paint on the finished product. This means he has to supervise our quality control, among other things. You know the expression?"

"Yes, I think so. It means that somebody has to check that everything is being done the way it's supposed to be done. Kind of a safeguard for you, and the customer both."

"Precisely. Now, I shall take you back four weeks. I had a letter of complaint from one of our customers in Canada. We cover the whole world, you see, and demand is growing. We've dealt with this Canadian company for some years, with very happy results, and I naturally took this complaint very seriously. They had taken delivery of one of our 4B tractors, and carried out a routine inspection. The 4B is one of our heaviest all-purpose machines, designed to work in some of the roughest terrain in the world, with minimum maintenance. The Canadians claimed that there was damage to the bodywork, of a very strange kind. There were several holes, of varying diameters, which seemed to serve no purpose. They sent photographs, to prove their point."

"I imagine you're bound to get occasional damage when you're shipping stuff all over the place," I suggested.

"Oh yes," he agreed, "but I'm not talking about damage, not in that sense. These holes were properly machined, and whoever made them intended them to be exactly where they were. The obvious assumption was that parts had somehow become confused in the assembly shop. In other words, the people in Canada hadn't got a proper 4B, but some kind of hybrid. This made it Dexter Hadley's problem, and he went through it thoroughly, without result. I wasn't prepared to accept that, so I went into it myself. The good name of this company rests on a reliable product, and it was no time to be studying other people's feelings. But there was no doubt about it, Hadley was right. There was no way that particular damage could have occured by accident."

He paused then, and I could tell we were getting to the nub of things. I felt I ought to demonstrate that I was listening.

"As I see it then," I contributed, "the holes were added after the assembly work was finished, which would mean one or two things. Either you have some kind of vandal loose in your own shop, or the holes were made after the tractor left here."

He seemed pleased with my effort.

"Exactly, Mr Preston. Quite so. As to the first solution, it did not take very long to eliminate the possibility.

Those holes needed special equipment, and they would take up several hours of time. If anyone wanted to vandalise any of our machines, they could do it more effectively inside five minutes, and the damage would not be visible to the naked eye. No, it emerged very quickly that the second solution had to be the correct one. Someone, for some reason, had tampered with the bodywork on that tractor after it left these premises."

I didn't see where all this was leading us. Things like this must be happening all the time, the way I saw it. It was a matter for an insurance company.

"Mr Weill," I said tentatively, "I hope you're not about to ask me to find out who punched holes in your tractor somewhere between here and Canada, because frankly — "

"Naturally not," and he sounded impatient. "Once I had the facts, I arranged for the shipment of an immediate replacement, the damaged one to be returned here as soon as possible. At that point, the whole business was no more than a tiresome nuisance, and I was prepared to write it off to experience. Hadley, and the production people, would carry out further investigations when we had the machine in our hands, but frankly I had little hope that we would ever find out what really happened. In fact, I put the whole business out of my mind, pending further reports. Then, last week, the returned 4B was off-loaded at the docks in Monkton City. It arrived the following day, and I may tell you there were five of the most senior people employed by this company waiting to receive it." He paused then, either for dramatic effect, or because he still couldn't quite bring himself to believe what he was saying. "Mr Preston, there were no holes on that tractor, no damage of any kind. It was as fine a product as we ever turned out."

Well, if he was in the business of surprising the audience, I would have to admit he was good at it.

"They could have been repaired, maybe?"

"Absolutely out of the question. The machine was immaculate." The expression on his face was slightly anxious, as though he were worried that I might not believe him.

"Mr Weill, this is a very odd story, but let me tell you the way it listens from this side. You know about tractors, that's your business. If you tell me the returned tractor was intact, O.K. there were no holes. To you it sounds crazy, but you'll be surprised to hear I don't think so. We've left the tractor business, which you know, and we're into the detective business, which I know. This sounds like the old switch game, Mr Weill, and it's been around since the flood."

He seemed relieved to realise that I wasn't going to query his story, but puzzled as to why.

"Switch game?" he echoed. "Just what is that?"

"It's the gold brick," I told him. "The peanut under the walnut shell, the three card dodge. Now you see it, now you don't. It's what the police call bunco. If your tractor had holes up in Canada, and no holes on its return, then we're talking about two tractors, Mr Weill. And I think your problem is more complicated than you realise. Mind if I smoke?"

I took out my Old Favorites, and looked at him enquiringly. He gestured impatiently for me to go ahead, saying.

"Of course, of course, but what do you mean by 'more complicated'?"

"I mean this. When the story opened, what you had was damage. Maybe somebody didn't like you, or your Canadian customer, so they vandalised the tractor. That's bad, but it was simple. It isn't so simple anymore. Whoever we're dealing with was in a position to switch the faulty machine for a good one, and that's a whole new can of worms. That means organisation, access to your stock, plus some kind of authority in the company structure. It also poses a question. Why should somebody go to all that trouble, simply to prevent you from looking at a few holes?"

He nodded, and obviously some of my reasoning must have already crossed his mind. He'd had days to think about it, compared to my minutes.

"Yes, I must say some of those things have occured to me, but I can't make any sense of it."

"So you had Dexter Hadley looking into it, and now he's dead," I suggested. "You're wondering if there could be any connection, and that's why we're having this chat. Right?"

The tiny eyes roved over me, while he pondered his reply.

"It seems ridiculous, I know. Clutching at straws, you may think. All the same, there is no denying the sequence. The company is somehow involved in this strange business with the tractor. Dexter Hadley was looking into it, and Dexter Hadley is dead.

One can't help feeling there could be a connection. Do you think I'm letting my imagination run away with me?"

I pulled my chin, thinking about it.

"Hard to say," I admitted. "It does sound crazy on the one hand, but then, so does making holes in tractors. I'd say your suspicion is no more wild than the facts. What did the police think about your theory?"

"The police?" and he looked horrified. "I didn't mention any of this to them. For one thing, I was still half-asleep when they told me what had happened, and the thought of connecting such a terrible thing with Dexter's job simply did not occur to me at the time."

"It's occurred to you now," I pointed out. "But you're still not talking to the law. You're talking to me. Why, Mr Weill?"

"Does it matter?" he countered.

"It matters to me," I assured him. "Concealment of information material to a case of murder is a very serious charge. They would love to catch me doing something like that. It could cost me my license, and a jail term of one to three years at the last count. If you want me to take this on, Mr Weill, you're going to have to give me a good cover story."

I settled back in the chair, prepared to be talked into it. What I'd said was true, but I didn't mind cutting a few corners. What I needed was for Weill to feed me a plausible story.

"Yes, yes I understand your position," he said thoughtfully. "Let us concentrate on the tractors, and put Hadley's unfortunate death to one side for the moment. I suspect some kind of elaborate fraud, although I can't imagine what it is. Suppose I hired you to investigate that, and only that? That would be well within your premise, I imagine?"

"Yes it would," I agreed, "but it would also look strange. The tractor thing has been going on for almost a week, and you don't seek outside help. Then Hadley comes to see me, Hadley gets murdered, and the very next day I'm on the company payroll. How's that going to look to an outsider?"

It was his turn to lean back, while he thought it over. I looked around for an ashtray, located one, and balanced it on my knee.

Finally he said.

"I think I have the answer, and I think you might like it. I've been considering calling in outside help, someone like yourself for the past few days. My fellow-directors here will confirm that — "

— I'll bet they will, I thought —

" — and then last night the problem was solved for me by your friend Randall. He told me about you, and you might be surprised to know that he spoke of you quite warmly."

"Randall did that?" I couldn't help the interruption.

"Yes. Oh, it wasn't voluntary. In fact I more or less forced it out of him. You see Mr Preston, and please don't be offended, when the sergeant told me Hadley had been to see you, I'm afraid I may have made some rather disparaging remarks about people in your line of work. Sergeant Randall reacted by telling me that whatever I might think, you were not some back-street operator. On the contrary, he said, they had worked with you many times in the past, and had never found you other than reliable. So, you see, I could claim that it was the police themselves who put your name into my mind."

Well, well, I reflected. If Randall had realised he was opening a door for me, he might have chosen his words more carefully.

"That sounds good," I admitted. "In fact, it sounds good enough. I will take the job, Mr Weill. But I have to tell you one thing. If it ties in with Dexter Hadley's death, I couldn't be too long in telling the police about it. Whatever they claim to think about me privately, they're still there to enforce the law. Where do we go from here?"

"I shall hand you over to a man named Walter Sturges. He is our Systems Manager, and familiar with every aspect of our work. It's his job to advise on alterations in methods and procedures. To do that, he has to understand the whole operation from the ground up."

"Then he would have worked closely with Dexter Hadley?"

"On occasion, yes. Before I call him up, there is one basic thing about this company which I have not yet mentioned. You are going to learn it anyway, and I should prefer it to come from me."

He stopped for a moment, as though to ensure I was paying attention. He needn't have concerned himself. I was almost on the edge of the chair. Why is it that so many people toss in the vital ingredient almost as an afterthought?

"Approximately one-third of the work-force," he continued slowly, "are men with criminal records. Ex-convicts. Most of the world turns its back on those people, but we do not. If we are satisfied that the man's crime was an isolated instance, and that he isn't a hardened criminal type, then we will give him a job. Overall, it works very well. There have only been three cases over the years where people have let us down. The majority are grateful for their chance, and they work hard to prove they are worthy of it. Not everyone in the outside world approves of our policy, Mr Preston, and that's another reason why I want to keep the police out of this affair until the last possible moment. They would be swarming all over these particular employees, and causing a lot of pointless hardship to them and their families. Do you understand?"

I ground out my cigaret, and got rid of the ashtray.

"I understand your motives Mr Weill," I assured him, "and they do you credit. All the same, I think you're going to have to be realistic about this. If there is something crooked going on in this organisation, the first people I shall be interested in will have to be the ones who've been in trouble before. I'd be sticking my head in the sand if I did anything else."

"Yes, I quite see that, and I expected it. But you will be acting from within, and you are not the police. There will be no harassment. This will be an internal investigation, and I shall ensure that people here understand they might be asked some questions. Innocent people won't take exception to that, not if they know the company is behind it. As for the guilty ones, if they exist, then the sooner we know about them the better."

It seemed a reasonable attitude, the way he put it. All the same, I had my reservations about the reception I might get, out among the men.

"How much will you tell Sturges?" I asked switching subjects. "Will he know that Hadley was a client of mine, for instance?"

He shook his head.

"No, I don't think that would be a very good idea. We don't deal in murder here. Our business is tractors and other equipment, and that's what you're here for, to look into our mystery. If you haven't any further questions, I'll ask Walt to come up."

And that was how I started in the tractor business.

4

ONE hour later I was sitting in the little office allocated to Walter Sturges, which was tucked away at the end of a cat-walk above the giant assembly shed. We had done the conducted tour of the premises, and I had been impressed by the wide range of knowledge of my guide.

Sturges was a six foot reed of a man, all bustling nervous energy, and with an enthusiasm for the job which would have been more understandable in someone aged twenty-five. He was forty-odd, and showed no signs of any comfortable slowing down.

"So what do you make of it, Mark?"

It had been Mark this and Walt that from the onset. I took another nip of my lemonade. It was a hell of a place for lemonade.

"Just this," I replied. "I don't see any way your 4B could have had those holes added on these premises. There are too many inspection checks along the way, too many different people involved. You wouldn't be dealing with one vandal, you'd need a whole conspiracy to do anything to one of these machines."

I jerked a thumb towards the window, which looked down on to the busy assembly floor. He nodded, pleased.

"That's the way I saw it, but it's good to have an independent confirmation. And, as I told you, once a piece of equipment is completed, it's taken off right away."

"Yes, you did tell me that," I agreed, "but we didn't go into the reasons. You have all this space here, plus a whole desert out there doing nothing. Why do you take things to this warehouse at the docks? It must be expensive. You have the building costs for one thing, a couple of extra employees in the place. Why?"

"Several reasons," he began. "For one thing, you're quite right about all the free parking we have here, but it can cost a lot of money and inconvenience just the same. There's the paint we use, for starters. It dries within a few hours, but it doesn't harden to the metal for three days. We found that the sun played hell with it inside twenty-four hours, and we had repaints on our hands. There's no way we could afford the space to keep them under shelter, so that was one problem. Another was the blaster, you know, these miniature sandstorms. They blow up every few weeks, and they don't last long, but they will strip new paint like a patent remover. One or two experiences like that in the early days, and the company realised they would need a warehouse. What with the increase in road haulage and air freight, there was a lot of available space dockside. The sensible thing was to rent some of it, rather than face the expense of building from scratch out here."

"Yes, I see what you mean. Well," I decided, "If those holes were punched in your 4B at this end of the line, it's my guess it was done in the warehouse."

He looked at me quizzically.

"Why do you say 'if'?" he queried. "Do you have any doubts about it?"

"Walt," I assured him, "I have doubts about everything. The holes make no sense, everyone's agreed on that. They could just as easily have been made in Vancouver as at this end. I'll go further. I'm still not satisfied there ever were any holes. Nobody down here has seen them. But I'm having to proceed on the assumption that they do exist, or did, and on that assumption I need to see the warehouse. Tell me about it. What kind of place is it?"

"Just a glorified shed," he shrugged. "After all, it doesn't have any purpose except to protect our stuff from the weather."

It was about what I'd expected.

"In your opinion then, it wouldn't

be impossible for somebody to get in there during the night, and make these alleged holes?"

He wagged his skull-like dome from side to side.

"No problem. An intelligent kid could get in, if he tried."

"Don't you have any security?"

"If you mean do we have our own force, no. It's not necessary. We share a community service with several other companies. The place is checked every couple of hours."

It seemed a rather casual way to be dealing with expensive agricultural equipment.

"How much does a 4B cost?" I asked him.

"When you say cost," he countered, "do you mean how much does it cost the company or how much does it cost to buy?"

"Market price," I qualified.

"Twenty four thousand, basic. There are a few refinements which can cost more."

Twenty four thousand. If anybody was playing tricks on Ag-Mach, using a switched tractor for the purpose, it was one hell of an expensive joke.

"So, at any one time, how much stuff would there be in the warehouse? I mean, how much in value?"

He made a face, thinking.

"Seldom less than a hundred thousand, I'd say. Often more. What's your point?"

"I'm thinking of going into the robbery business," I told him frankly. "The way you tell it, all I have to do is drive up to the place, steal all the machines, and drive away. Or did I miss something?"

"Only the practicalities," he grinned. "You'd need three or four giant lo-load haulers, plus drivers. A convoy. Plus, you'd need all the lights switched on. Plus, you'd have to have three or four hours uninterrupted work. The scale of the operation beats you before you get started. It's a far cry from heisting a couple of television sets in the boot of a car. And, don't forget, the insurance people have taken a good close look at things, and they're happy to carry the cover. I don't have to tell you how fussy those boys are."

When he explained it like that, I could see the sense of it.

"Maybe I'll stick to television sets," I conceded. "All right, so I can't steal your property, but I could make holes in it, yes?"

"You could," he agreed sadly. "I don't see why you'd want to, but you could."

"I'll get over there, and take a look around. Who do I talk to?"

"Man named Jenks, Sam Jenks. I'll phone ahead and tell him to expect you some time."

"Thanks."

It was on the tip of my tongue to ask whether Jenks was one of the ex-convicts on the payroll, but I decided against it. Time enough for that later, if it seemed necessary. I was on the point of leaving when the curved ball sailed over his desk.

"How do you see this tying in with the Hadley murder?"

The delivery was so casual I almost struck out.

"Why should there be any connection at all?" I parried.

"Aw, come on, Mark, you're the big detective, not me. One day, old Dex gets himself killed, the very next day you turn up here asking questions."

I looked at him seriously, shaking my head.

"I am here to look into this damaged 4B," I assured him. "As to the Hadley murder, I know nothing about it, and I don't want to. That is police business, and I'm just a private badge. Let me tell you something. Murder is off my territory. If I were to start poking around on a murder investigation, the police would stake me out on an anthill. You won't find a private operator in the state who'll stick his nose into a homicide. That's O.K. on tee-vee, but not in the big world, so forget it."

It all sounded straightforward and sincere, or so I hoped. Sturges held my open gaze for a few seconds, then nodded.

"Yes. I guess so. See what you mean."

I couldn't tell whether he was really convinced, but at least he dropped the subject. There was one last subject I wanted to touch on.

"From what I gather, Mr Weill seems to put a lot of trust in Mrs Fordyce. She knows everything that goes on here, and that makes her a valuable source of information. What's your assessment of her?"

He snorted and grinned, all at once.

"The ice-lady? Believe me, information is safe with that one. If you were to say it was a nice day, she'd check with the boss before she agreed with you. The original clam from Clamsville."

"What about her husband? Does he work at the plant?"

"There isn't any husband, not any more. She was already divorced when she came here, three, four years ago. So she claims. The popular theory is that she froze him to death."

I grinned back at him, glad to be back on the familiar ground of manly confidences.

"If I read you right, the lady is not exactly the swinging hostess of the company?"

"You got it. Hands off, do not touch, this is a restricted area. If you want to check our people, leave her till last."

I had some private reservations about that, but they had nothing to do with the case. I thanked him again, told him I'd be in touch, and went back to the administration building. Margaret Fordyce seemed surprised to see me, when I walked into her little private office.

"Mr Preston, I'd no idea you were still here," she exclaimed "I'm afraid Mr Weill will be tied up for the next couple of hours."

"That's O.K. it's you I came to see."

"Oh." She put down the papers she'd been studying, and studied me instead. "Naturally, anything I can do — "

She left it unfinished, but she wasn't the kind of woman who was inviting suggestive replies. I thought an official-sounding phrase would help.

"It's the report-procedure," I explained. "I have to get that clear before I leave."

That produced a look a faint puzzlement, and she tipped her head to one side enquiringly.

"I imagine you will simply deal with Mr Weill direct."

"Naturally," I confirmed, "but I can't be bothering him with every interim stage. The plant only works office hours, but that doesn't apply in the investigation business. I have to have a number I can call at any time. If I find it's necessary to go up to Vancouver, for example, I shall just go. But I have to be able to tell somebody. It must be someone close to Mr Weill, and who knows about me already. I was wondering about you."

I kept my expression dead-pan. She seemed half-convinced.

"Well," she replied thoughtfully, "I imagine there's no harm in that. Very well. You can call this number, if there's any real necessity, but I must ask you to keep it confidential. You won't find it in the directory, because it's unlisted, and that's the way I intend it to remain."

She was all crisp and business-like as she scribbled the number on a pad, tore off the sheet and handed it to me. I tucked it in my pocket, well aware that this was not the time to break procedure.

"Thank you," I acknowledged. "I'm just on my way to your warehouse at the docks. I don't expect to come up with anything right away, but perhaps you'd let Mr Weill know what I'm doing?"

It seemed to strike the right note, and she nodded agreement. She even managed a small joke.

"I suppose it isn't every day you're engaged to look for holes?"

"Especially disappearing holes," I confirmed. "Still, life is full of surprises. That's why I do this job. You never can tell what's going to come up next. I'll be in touch."

Our respective nods were formal enough, but there was something lurking in her inspecting eyes which I couldn't pin down.

Not then.

★ ★ ★

The dock area is fed by two main arteries. The coastal highway to the north, where it links the old Six Six, and south, where it leads to San Diego, is the road to use if you want to avoid the city. Otherwise there is no alternative to Conquest Street, which heads smack into the center of town. Local historians will tell you that the name is a corruption of the title originally given to this highway by our Spanish predecessors, who named it after the Conquistadors, and they could be right for all I know. According to which history you choose to believe, those old-time pioneers were either daring, adventurous trail-blazers, or as fine a bunch of cut-throats as ever graced our shores, with a thousand miles of murder, rape and carnage behind them. Conquest Street itself is a similar distillation of good and bad. It starts off in the business section, with a legitimate theater right on the corner with Fourth, then come a sprinkling of business houses, interspersed with a few good restaurants. After that, there is a gradual deterioration in occupancy. First come the bucket-shops and the fast food outlets, then the sharp operators and the greasy spoons. After that, the place is wide open, a pestilence of stag shows, blue movies, jazz cellars and beer parlors. Gin-joints and sin-joints, betting places and petting places, you name it, we do it. Twelve Exotic Girls, Count 'Em, step right in, Swedish Massage by Rosita — (Swedish?) — Special Poses. Every sense is assailed and affronted by the glaring lights, the blaring, jangling music, and the hundred powerful aromas, from every style of ethnic cooking, cheap perfume and sweat. At the bottom end, and the term is used advisedly, comes the dock area. Conquest ends just short of the waterfront, breaking up into a dribble of lesser thoroughfares like River Street, Crane Street and so forth. This had been my territory when I first went into the private eye business, and I knew it well, but hadn't been that way for some time. The address of the Ag-Mach warehouse was off Crane Street, where a number of disused sheds were a monument to earlier days, when Monkton had been an important cargoport. There was still a certain amount of traffic, but it was nothing like it had been in its heyday.

In earlier days, every company had its

own security police, but there was no longer any justification for that. Instead, simple fences had been erected between the sheds, denying access except at certain entry-roads, where guards could control the traffic movement. It was an inexpensive way to police the area, but effective. I showed a bored man in a gray uniform the pass I'd been given by Walter Sturges, and he pretended to inspect it, waving me through. Shed Fourteen was clearly marked by huge white stencilled numbers, which had been newly painted, causing it to stand out from its neighbours. There were two cars parked outside, and I pulled in beside them, looking around for a door. Before I was out of the car, a man emerged from a small doorway I hadn't spotted, and waited for me to approach.

He wore a rough woollen work-shirt, despite the heat, and a pair of stained jeans. As I approached, he nodded.

"You'll be Mr Preston," he greeted.

"They told me you were coming. I'm Sam Jenks."

He didn't offer to shake hands, but his gravelly tone was not unfriendly.

"I'm Preston," I confirmed. "Mind showing me around, Sam?"

"You can see what there is," he agreed. "It ain't much, but you're welcome to it."

We went inside, and he closed the door. Two things struck me at once. The darkness, and the cold. Next time, I'd dig out a work-shirt of my own.

"Wait a minute, I forgot we'd need the lights, you being new."

He clicked a switch behind me, and a half-a-dozen lights sprang to life, giving just sufficient illumination for me to examine the place. The shed was about a hundred feet long by sixty, with a roof about forty feet above my head. At one end stood a brand-new earth mover, flanked by a couple of small tractors. The place was otherwise a simple shell, except for a lean-to hut which was stuck in one corner.

That was obviously where Jenks and the other man passed their time.

"Ain't much, is it?" queried my guide.

"No," I agreed. "Is it always this cold?"

"'Cept in the winter," he confirmed. "Then, it's colder. It's the insulation, you see. This place was built to hold anything, and time was there'd be stuff coming in, like food and such, which could rot. It ain't like a real refrigerated place, but it's cold enough."

That would be why there were no window spaces. The place was the nearest they could build to a giant ice-box. I shivered.

"How do you guys stand this?" I queried.

Jenks laughed.

"We don't have to," he replied. "We got our own shed, right there, and that's where you'll find us. Come on, I'll show you."

He led me down to the indoor shack, and motioned me quickly inside. The temperature must have risen twenty degrees at once, and a second man sat in a padded chair watching our entrance.

"This here's Mr Preston they told us about," announced Jenks. "Meet my partner, Al Genette."

Genette was about thirty, and looked Italian. He inclined his head, and seemed friendly enough. There was a television set against one wall, coffee pot and makings, while the table boasted a greasy deck of cards, and a checkerboard.

"Not much for you to do all day," I offered.

"On a busy day we don't have much to do," corrected Jenks, "other days, like now, there's nothing at all. Where do you want to start the search?"

"Search?" I looked at him in surprise.

"Sure," he replied, deadpan. "You come here to find them missing holes, didn't you? From that 4B tractor?"

Jokes, yet.

"They could be anywhere," I

shrugged. "For all I know, you boys could have dug a hole and buried 'em. Do you have any tools here?"

"You mean like shovels? No. Nothing like that," Jenks was still on that hole joke. Then he looked more serious. "Why what's up? Something wrong with your car? Might be a coupla screwdrivers around someplace?"

"The car's fine," I assured him. "No, I was thinking more about power-tools. Like a drill, for instance."

They exchanged glances, and some of the friendliness left the room.

"You think we done it, is that it?" demanded Genette.

I held up my hands for peace.

"Certainly not, I'm not accusing you of anything. It's just that somebody had to make those holes, and that means they had something to do it with. If there's no drill here, they must have brought their own. How would they get in, by the way? I imagine you lock that door?"

"Sure we lock it," protested Jenks.

"Key stays right in my pocket the whole time."

"T'ain't the only key, though," reminded Genette. "There's one back at the plant, and Mr Hadley always had his own."

It was no more than I expected. Once there is more than one key in existence, there might as well be a hundred, in my experience.

"If somebody came in here during the night, I imagine you'd spot it, wouldn't you? I mean, they'd leave Indian signs of some kind."

"Hard to say," mused Genette. "We'd spot it fast enough if people came in here, using our stuff, but if they stayed outside, just drilling holes, I don't know."

I hadn't expected to learn anything from the visit, and that's the way it was turning out. My main purpose had been to get the feel of the place. There was only one more area to explore.

"Tell me what happens when stuff

is shipped out," I asked. "You get word from the plant, and then what happens?"

"Depends," said Jenks, very much the senior man. "If it's a daylight job, Al and me do the work, with one of the customer's agents watching. If it's night-time, the customer supplies the labour, and somebody from the plant does the watching. Don't ask me why we do it different. I got my own ideas."

He closed his mouth tight, and his ideas stayed on the other side. Pity. I would have liked to hear what was on his mind. Genette filled the gap.

"Sam don't wanna tell you, but I will. You see, after five o'clock we get paid double, and we figure the company's holding out on us."

The last thing I needed was to get involved in a labour dispute.

"I'm the wrong man to be talking to," I reminded them. "You need somebody like Mr Sturges."

"You may be right," conceded

Genette. "Especially since Hadley is dead."

My ears pricked up at the mention of my murdered client.

"What did Mr Hadley have to do with it?" I asked, trying to sound casual.

"It was him changed the system, coupla months back," grumbled Jenks. "Up till then, Al and me used to do the night loading."

"Did he give any reason," I persisted.

"Oh sure," he scoffed. "Gobbledegook, that's what he give us. Something about insurance."

"Insurance?" I encouraged, but Jenks lapsed again into silence.

Al Genette came again to the rescue.

"The way it was told us," he explained, "the company insurance covers this place all the time, but movements out are only covered in working time, that is up to five o'clock. After that, if we move stuff and it gets lost, the insurance company won't pay."

"But," I concluded, "if the customer shifts it out himself, that's O.K. because he has separate cover."

Genette nodded.

"That's the way it got told us," he confirmed.

I wondered about it, but it was no use pursuing an insurance problem with these two characters. Instead I passed out the Old Favorites, and we all lit up.

"I know you men have been all through this twenty times before," I opened carefully, "but it's all new to me. Would you mind telling me what happened the day the damaged 4B came back from Canada?"

They looked at each other in mutual resignation, and Jenks replied.

"Nothing happened," he grunted. "We come into work, like always, and there she was, just sitting there. Not a mark on her. That was eight in the a.m. Around eight-thirty, Mr Weill turns up hisself, with Mr Hadley and Mr Sturges, plus a couple of other guys from the plant. That's all that happened."

Drawing information out of these people was a slow process.

"You said she was there when you came into work," I reminded. "What I really want to know is what happened when she first arrived."

Jenks looked perplexed, wrinkling up his face like a worried gnome.

"How would we know that? We wasn't here. She come in around midnight or so. Tell you the truth we was surprised to see her. We thought at first it was the other one, still there."

The other one. If Jenks ever got around to writing a rhapsody, it wouldn't sound as sweet as those words.

"You mean you left a 4B here in the shed the night before?"

"I'm telling you, ain't I? We knew this other one would be shipped out during the night. Give us a surprise when we found it hadn't gone. Then, when we come in here, we found the papers on the desk." He waved a hand at the coffee stained table with the checkerboard. "The first one had been taken all right, but the other one, the one they had said was damaged, that come in it's place."

I nodded. Suddenly, the freight papers became more important than the actual equipment.

"These papers," I asked gently, "don't they have to be signed by somebody from Ag-Mach?"

"Sure they do. Natcherly. They was all according to Hoyle. Mr Hadley was here personal. I know his signature all right."

"Of course you do," I soothed. "What about the times? Do they put times on these papers?"

The two warehousemen stared at each other, trying to understand what I was driving at. This time it was Genette who took up the running.

"You don't know much about shipping, do you?" he scoffed. "You can just bet there are times on those sheets."

Better and better. I grinned, to show there was no offense.

"I told you I was new to this. Do you happen to recall what the times were? I mean, what time did the new one go out, for starters."

"Ten o'clock," stated Jenks. "It was right there in the sheets."

"That's right," confirmed Genette, "and the one down from Canada was marked in for two a.m. What are you driving at, mister?"

I shook my head in disappointment. The timing of the two moves did not match up to my hopes. It would have been so simple if both the 4Bs had been in the shed at the same time. That way, the one from Canada could mistakenly have been taken during the night hours. As things stood, there had been no room for error.

Genette was still waiting for me to reply.

"Damned if I know," I told him

honestly. "I'm just digging around, hoping something will turn up."

"Take my advice and forget it," suggested Jenks. "Believe me, we been over this fifty ways from Christmas, and there's one road out, just one. There ain't no holes, there never was no holes. This whole thing is just some kinda crazy stunt. You can take my word, that is the bottom line. Right, Al?"

He turned to his partner for support, and was rewarded with a decisive nod.

"He's telling it, Mr Preston. I ain't no genius, but I guess I know a hole when I see one."

"Right," chimed Jenks, "and when we don't see one, too."

His grammatical follow-through was arguable, but I knew what he intended to say. They'd both peeked at their watches in the last few minutes, and I sensed they were anxious to be rid of me, so they could lock up for the night. I made for the door.

"Nothing here for me," I decided.

"Thank you for the co-operation. The man I would have liked to talk to about all this was Mr Hadley. Terrible thing, him getting killed that way. What kind of man was he?"

Jenks looked towards Genette to answer me. It seemed, from my brief visit, that although he was senior on the payroll, he deferred to the younger man when it came to matters involving the think-process.

"He always treated us decent," pronounced Genette. "Been a bit snappy lately, but I guess we all have our off-days."

"The business with the holes probably played on his mind," I suggested. "Must have worried him quite a lot."

"Yeah, but even before that he's been kinda edgy," supplied Genette. "We thought maybe he was sick or something. Always in and out, picking on this and that. He never used to be that way."

"You ask me, it was ulcers," pronounced Jenks. "Seen it before in

110

these young guys. They take on all these responsibilities, all these pressures, they figure there's nothing they can't do. Next thing you know, ulcers. I seen it before."

He nodded mysteriously, and Genette seemed to agree with him. When it came to knowledge of the world, and, in particular, grave medical disorders, the delicate balance of power between these two evidently shifted in favor of the older man. There was nothing to be gained by arguing the point.

"Could be," I assented. "Ulcers can play the devil with a man's temper."

We all inclined our heads, the three wise men of medicine, united in our diagnosis.

"Well," I said heartily, "thanks again. I'll leave you to it. Don't forget, if you happen to find a pile of holes — "

" — you'll be the first to know," confirmed Genette, grinning.

Jenks merely looked puzzled.

5

IT was almost five-thirty when I made it back to the office, and Florence Digby had already left for home. She'd left the place neat, as always, and my desk presented its normal immaculate appearance, uncluttered by any signs of work, except for one typed note square in the middle.

Mr Steiner called twice!

What could he want? Shad Steiner is the night-editor of the Monkton City Globe, and one of the coast's great newspapermen. In his middle fifties, Shad had a worried lined face which could easily have belonged to a man twice his age, but the mental processes behind it were razor-sharp. The fourth estate have a great catch-phrase, which they tend to use when convenient, and overlook when prudence intervenes.

'Publish and be damned', that's what they say, but they don't always adhere to it. Steiner does, and always has. He'd published, and been damned by every crooked administration in the paper's history. The crooks came and went, but Steiner and the Globe stayed. He'd probably been responsible for clearing up more of the city's garbage than half-a-dozen of the so-called Reform Committees. Their aim was usually quite simple. What they said was, 'Let's get rid of these corrupt officials.' What they meant was, 'let's replace them with our own corrupt officials,' but they normally showed a certain natural reticence about the second principle. Steiner had no such inhibitions, and if you care to check on any politician's early morning reading, you will invariably find that day's edition of the Globe resting on top of the pile.

I was interested to know what he wanted with me, but I had some reservations about finding out. There was still a personal matter to be resolved with the features editor of that fine organ, a certain Mike Blair, and I didn't want to see that lady on her own ground. We had a situation which required delicate handling, preferably against a background of soft lights and sweet music. She was going to be hard enough to persuade, even with all the trappings. In the hurly burly of her professional surroundings, I was on a loser.

Sitting at the desk, I stared out at the blue early evening sky, hoping for a sign. There wasn't even a cloud I could interpret. If Steiner had called once, I might have let it go. But twice? I knew the set-up at the Globe, and I knew he was in the middle of his busiest period of the day, and yet he found time to call me twice. Reluctantly, I admitted to myself what I'd known from the outset. I was going to have to return his call.

Picking up the handset I pushed buttons, and asked the cheerful girl on the switchboard to put me through.

"Shad, how are you? This is Preston. They tell me you've been trying to contact me."

It was good, business-like stuff. Frank and open. It was rewarded with a surly grunt.

"How I am is busy," he told me. "You think this sheet puts itself together? Got something for you, Preston. Are you coming?"

I hesitated.

"Couldn't we talk about it on the telephone," I hedged.

"We could not," he said decisively. "You coming or not? Last call."

"I'm coming," I agreed sadly.

It isn't easy trying to park a car outside a newspaper office at that time of evening. Most of the delivery trucks are there, plus all the reporting staff cars, because this is put-to-bed time. Inside, the place was a seething mass of people, all talking across each other, shouting into telephones, scurrying around on mysterious errands. To one side was the small glass cubicle which was the hub of the whole machine, the night editor's office. When I walked in, he was deep in concentration.

"This'll have to go on Three," he decided. "It's too good to bury."

A forty year old man in his shirt-sleeves knitted his brow and leaned on the desk.

"But the building contract story — " he began.

" — will have to move," interrupted Steiner. "This new story is hot. Re-page, Mo."

Mo nodded, straightened up, and went out, looking at me curiously.

"What's this hot new story on page three?" I queried.

"Buy a paper," snapped Steiner. "Glad you could make it, Preston. Wait a minute."

He flicked a switch and bellowed into a black box.

"Where are these pictures for the spread?" he growled. "Do I have to come and get 'em?"

"Ten minutes, Mr Steiner," crackled the box.

"Eight," he corrected, switching off.

Then he leaned back and subjected me to one of his suspicious glares.

"What's going down, Preston?"

"We're going to have to re-page the building contract story," I replied.

He sighed, running a hand covered with black wiry hair over his worn features.

"And they wonder why vaudeville died," he emitted sadly. "You, Mr Smart-Ass Preston, are on to something, and I want to know what it is. Or do I have to threaten you?"

I made the mistake of not knowing what he meant.

"Threaten me," I suggested.

"O.K. How's this for a bottom of Page One? 'Why are police taking no action on mysterious doings of well-known private investigator? Preston, engaged on secret work for Ag-Mach Company, was last person to see company official Dexter Hadley alive.

117

Hadley, whose bullet-riddled body was discovered' — do you want to hear more?"

"No," I admitted. "Who says I'm working for Ag-Mach?"

"Do you want to deny it?"

"No, but I'd prefer to keep it quiet. What are you up to, Shad?"

"This here is what we call a newspaper," he said softly. "We print stories about what's going on in the world. Last night, you stood up a certain young woman, a very choice specimen of the breed. That is not like you, Preston. It's what people call uncharacteristic. The young woman is very upset, and I have cause to know, because she has been bending my ear with some very choice thoughts about what ought to be done to you. That's point one. Point two is, you couldn't keep the appointment because a nasty policeman took you away. This man wanted to know why your name was in the pocket of another man who'd just been murdered. Now it turns out

118

you are working for the dead man's employers, and that is point three. There's a very bad smell around, and I want to turn it into newsprint. You want to give it to a reporter, or just talk?"

I sat down, chewing on my lower lip. It was no surprise that he should know why I'd been down to headquarters. There's always somebody around who feeds the papers little titbits like that. Evidently, there had been someone out at the Ag-Mach plant who also thought I was worth a phone-call. The situation wasn't good. I couldn't hope to keep my assignment for the company a big secret forever, but that wasn't what bothered me. If the Globe chose to mix all the facts together, and slant the wording in a certain way, I could be made to look bad to Rourke and Randall.

"Why are you doing this?" I asked him.

He shrugged.

"Anything for a story. Besides, I'm

jealous about Mike Blair. If I was ten years younger — "

"Horsefeathers," I cut in. "You never were ten years younger. Even if you were, Rachel would nail you to the wall. This isn't like you, Shad. It's what some people would call uncharacteristic. What's the pitch?"

Because there had to be one. I'd known the man too long to believe he'd suddenly joined the blackmail squad. Suddenly, he winked.

"A small favor."

"Hell, I'd have done you a favor without all this chatter," I reminded him. "What is it?"

"A few months ago, a young couple moved into a house not far from where I live. Name of Palmer, seemed like a nice people. Rachel used to talk to the wife a little bit, you know how these things are."

I nodded, to indicate I knew how those things were.

"And?"

"Then, a few weeks back, the young

feller got himself killed in a car accident. Terrible business. He was just twenty-eight years old. They said he was drunk when he did it."

"Tough," I agreed, "but these things happen."

"They do, they do," he wagged his head philosophically. "Except that the young man didn't drink hardly at all. A glass of wine at Christmas, one of those guys."

"If that's the way he was," I pointed out, "then he'd be all the more likely to have an accident when he broke his rule. He wouldn't know how to handle it."

He waved at me to stop interrupting.

"I know all that, and I agree with you. There's more. Rachel tried to comfort the widow. She was all alone in the world, no family to speak of. Then, a week after the funeral, she ups and leaves. Moved away, and didn't even say where. Now, I've seen a lot of grief in my time, and I wish I had a nickel for every woman who quit the neighbourhood after her husband died. I told Rachel to forget it. She thought there was something not quite kosher going on, and I have to admit, when she gets these little bees in her bonnet, it turns out she's right more often than not. Still, this time was the exception, I told her, and we dropped the subject."

He stopped talking for a moment, and I thought the story was over.

"Well, that is a sad tale, Shad, but I don't see where it gets us."

"I'm not through yet," he persisted nastily. "Was a time when people didn't interrupt their elders. Now then, to bring it up to date. Last week, Rachel went to meet a friend for coffee. The waitress turned out to be this young widow friend of hers. Naturally, Rachel was glad to see her, but it wasn't mutual. The girl practically snubbed her, and I may tell you, Rachel was very upset."

"I can imagine," I consoled, "but maybe the girl wanted to start a new life, forget all the past. It would be understandable."

He nodded his emphatic agreement.

"Exactly what I told her," he stated. "Put the whole affair out of your mind, I said. Let the young woman get on with her new life. And that's where it rested, until Gil Randall snatched you away from Mike Blair last night."

He was going too fast for me now, and I stared at him blankly.

"All right," I conceded, "you lost me. What's the connection?"

I had to wait to find out, because at that moment an irate reporter came barging in, wanting to know why his story had been left out of the next day's issue. While they were arguing, I reviewed what Steiner had told me so far. It all seemed harmless to me, as stories go. Finally, the interrupter went away and Shad frowned as he brought his thoughts back to me.

"Ah yes," he recalled, "you were asking me what the connection was. Just this. The young man who died in the car-crash, he worked for this company of yours, Ag-Mach. There's more. His boss was Dexter Hadley, and I know that for a fact, because he attended the funeral. Are you getting all this?"

He needn't have been concerned. I was getting it all right.

"In spades," I assured him. "It's a strange coincidence, I'll give you that. So what's this favor?"

Steiner clicked his teeth impatiently.

"In spades is a bridge term," he reminded me. "What you're trying to play is poker. Couldn't you look just a little bit interested?"

"I'm interested," I admitted, "but I'm not going to make a big drama out of it. I don't see how you can make a connection between some drunk driver killing himself, and his boss getting himself murdered. Too far-fetched."

"Just the same," he persisted, "that's the favor. What harm can it do, for you just to ask a few questions? There might be something there, after all.

If there is, then it's me doing you a favor."

I don't like it when people put the pressure on.

"Why don't you leave it to the police?" I asked him. "They'll be on to it fast enough if there's anything to connect the two things."

"Ah," and he raised a triumphant finger. "You are not thinking, Preston. Not thinking at all. Why should Homicide be interested? They never heard of Larry. That was the young feller's name, Larry. There was no suggestion of any homicide, so the case was dealt with by the local precinct. You have a clear field."

And a barren one, I reflected. In my own mind, I doubted whether Steiner would really carry out his threat of printing a yarn about me, but there was no point in putting him to the test.

"Larry Palmer, you say? What was his job?"

"Some kind of design draughtsman," he replied.

"A design man? But Hadley was a finance genius. I wouldn't have thought he'd have a draughtsman on his staff. That's the technical side."

Steiner shrugged.

"I wouldn't know about that. All I know is, Hadley was the one who handled everything for the widow. A real nice man, she said."

There was no future in pursuing that line, since neither of us was in possession of the facts.

"Let's talk about the widow," I suggested. "What's her name, and where was this restaurant?"

"Suzanne," he supplied, "and the place is near you, over on the Heights. Called the Coffee-Shop."

I knew it well, and it was only a few blocks from Parkside.

"You wouldn't happen to know what her name was before she got married?" I queried. "Reason I ask is, women sometimes change their names in these situations, and usually they just go back to the one they started out with."

He shook his head.

"I wouldn't know that," he denied.

"How about a picture?" I pressed. "Maybe you ran one with the story about her husband's accident."

"Yes, I believe we did. We'll soon know." He did some more barking into the black box, and someone at the other end got busy. Then he stared at me, thinking. "You know, I'm changing my mind."

"What about?"

"The more I think about it, the less I consider this a favor. I'm getting the feeling it's me doing the favor."

"We'll see. Anyway, I'll take a look at it, and tell you what comes out."

"That you will," he nodded. "In fact, I think we ought to keep the whole thing in the family."

I didn't like the ring of it.

"What whole thing?"

"The story, when you get it. Let's make it a Globe exclusive. You can be like our man at the scene."

Now, he was pushing too hard.

"Your man at the scene gets paid, doesn't he?"

His eyes twinkled. No, glittered. Glittered is harder.

"Oh, I'll pay you," he promised.

"How much?"

Now he looked upwards for top-level reference.

"People nowadays, all they think of is money. For you, I can do better. I can square you with a certain features editor. You should pay me money."

It was a tempting offer, and I gave in.

"I'll do what I can."

That door was open again, and a worried looking girl rushed in, holding out a glossy picture to Steiner. He took it, looking at his watch.

"Four minutes," he groused. "When I was down there, I would have been fired if I didn't do it in two."

Uncertain of whether he was kidding or not, she gave a nervous smile and made her escape. I winked at her as she went, to show it was all a gag.

"Here. This is Suzanne Palmer. For once, we got a good likeness."

It was a head and shoulders of a healthy looking girl in her middle twenties, all blonde hair and tan, little make-up. You could see a hundred like her on any California beach. There was a photo-copy of the report on her husband's death attached to the picture, and I scanned it quickly, learning nothing relevant.

"Thanks," I slipped the photograph into my pocket. "Well, I'd better get out there and start chasing my tail. You'll be wanting to get on with bullying people."

"Keeps me young," he asserted. "Let me know how it comes out."

I made my way through the busy office, keeping a wary eye out for Mike Blair, and was thankful to make a clean exit. Once I'd negotiated the car out of the crowded lot, I headed back across town to Sam's Place, one of my favorite watering holes. What I needed was a few minutes to myself for a quiet think, and I find I can do it in Sam's. The place is always busy, but a man is left alone if that's how he wants it, and that suited me. I had just picked up my cold mug of beer, and was looking around for a haven, when a familiar voice grumbled in my ear.

"Now you want me, now you don't."

I turned my head, to see the lugubrious features of Sam Thompson. Without my being aware of it, he'd been lurking at the back of my mind, and the sight of him crystallised my thoughts.

"Glad you're here, let's find a seat."

The only available space was at a table where two horse-players were deep in discussion about track matters, and I would have been glad to eavesdrop in the ordinary way. When it comes to the ponies, you never know where you might pick up that vital piece of information. As it was, I knew our own conversation was safe. These two characters were away into their own world, and they had no time to waste on anyone else's affairs.

Just the same, we kept our voices low.

"They tell me you're going to retire, and buy your own stable."

"Ha ha," I returned sourly. "All I won was a few hundred."

"That's not the way the story goes. The fat part of fifty grand was the last I heard."

He blinked at me owlishly, and I shook my head impatiently. At this rate, if the rumour kept on growing at the same pace, I'd be buying the Palmtrees track outright.

"Then you heard wrong. I'm still working, and that's what I want to talk to you about. Did you read about the killing last night? Man named Dexter Hadley? He was dumped on a vacant lot near the docks."

"I seen it on the news," he confirmed. "What about it?"

"He was my client," I explained. "He wanted me to check up on what his wife was doing, and that was why I wanted you in the first place. Then, he got himself killed, and that was the end of it. That's why you got cancelled."

"It's too bad," he grumbled, "I'm a little short on bread at this point in time. Did the wife knock him off?"

"Not unless she carries two different weapons with her. Anyway, things have changed again, and I'm back on the case. I want you to take a look at the lady, find out what's going on, if anything."

He nodded, sipping at his beer, and wiping suds away from his chin.

"Only thing is," he demurred, "if the husband is dead, who meets the tab?"

Thompson has a very practical turn of mind.

"In your case, I do," I assured him. "And that's all you need to know."

I proceeded to fill in such information as I had about Joyce who shall be known as Rosanna, Hadley. Outside of that, I told him nothing. There was no mention of tractors with holes in, nothing about Ag-Mach, and especially nothing about the latest development, which was the previous death of Larry Palmer. If Thompson was going to take an interest in Hadley's widow, it was just possible that the homicide people would take an interest in Thompson. If that should happen, then the least he knew the better. When I'd given him all he needed to know, he asked a few supplementaries, and then said.

"When do I start?"

"As of now. Things sometimes snowball fast after a murder has been committed, and I don't want to have to read about them in the newspapers. Any reason you can't get on it right away?"

"There'll be expenses," he reminded me. "Taxis and such. Like I said, there's a bread famine right at this moment."

I gave him fifty dollars, and told him to spread it thin. As he went out, I speculated about whether I was throwing my money away, and decided I probably was. Still, if it hadn't been for Hadley's concern about his wife's activities, I would never have made the team in the first place. It would be tidier all around for me to know about that lady, and, after all, the man had paid me the five hundred.

Maybe I should do something to earn it.

6

WITH Thompson gone, I went to the row of pay-phones at the rear of the bar, picking over my change. I had to wait while a tubby red-faced man explained to his wife that he'd been caught up in an unexpected conference at the office, and would be late getting home. Then he spent some time listening to the opinions being expressed at the other end, the red face turning to puce and finally deep mauve. It sounded to me as if he'd had this same conversation not a few times before, and Mrs Tubby wasn't buying the unexpected conference. Finally, he got mad, and said a few words that no lady should have to hear, and slammed the phone down. Then he glared at me, to see whether I had anything to say, but I made a great show of sorting through my coins.

Margaret Fordyce answered on the third ring. When she heard who was calling, she didn't exactly bubble with girlish enthusiasm.

"Mr Preston, I thought I had made it perfectly clear that I only expected you to call this number if the circumstances warranted."

"Oh they do," I assured her hastily. "They certainly warrant. I need two pieces of information, if you can help me. First, I want the insurance company which covers the shipment of Ag-Mach products. Do you happen to know it?"

There was a pause while she digested the first question.

"It's Amalgamated National," she replied finally, "and they close down at five o'clock, just like everyone else, so that one could have waited till tomorrow morning. What's your other question?"

She was pushing the prim school teacher act too hard.

"Let's just stay with the first one," I suggested. "The office may close at five but if you think that's the end of it, you don't know much about insurance. Those guys never sleep. I need the name of the man who handles your business, if you know it."

"His name is Furst," she replied unwillingly. "That's F-U-R-S-T, first name Jed. The only number I would have is the office number."

This last seemed to be delivered with quiet triumph, as though we were in some kind of contest.

"Thank you, I'll take it from there. You see, us big detectives have special access to all kinds of information. We call one source the telephone book, and there won't be too many people named F-U-R-S-T." I was beginning to sound as difficult as she was. "Now the other one is easy. I'd like Walter Sturges home number, if you have it."

"Just a moment."

It seemed to me the bang in my ear as she rested the receiver was louder than it needed to be. After a few seconds she was back.

"I have Mr Sturges number now."

I scribbled it down, and thanked her.

"Is that all?" she asked.

"Why, yes."

"In that case, I'm sorry. It's just that I seem to spend so much of my time fending off — well — I think you know what I mean."

A chink in the armour, yet. The change in her attitude carried with it a softer tone, which suited my image of her far better.

"Lady, I know exactly what you mean, and say no more. Thanks for the information, it'll be a big help."

Everybody thanked everybody else, and I broke the connection, then dialled the Sturges number. I allowed him one dozen burrs before deciding he wasn't going to answer. Then I tried Information and they came up with two numbers which could be my Mr Furst. One of them answered on the second ring, and assured me he was in the ironmongery business. From the second number there was no reply, and I was beginning to feel frustrated. No Sturges and no Furst. Maybe there was a conspiracy. They couldn't answer their home telephones because they were together someplace, comparing notes. Better yet, they were dreaming up some new method of producing phantom holes in tractors.

A voice behind me grumbled about people spending all night on the telephone. I'd already tried four calls, so the man had a point. I fished in the coin slot, just in case, and came up with a dime. Good. Then I went back in the bar and stood there, uncertain of my next move. I was up against my usual dilemma between Rules One and Four of the investigating business. Rule One says 'When in doubt, rush out and slug somebody'. On the other hand, Rule Four says 'Hasty action is no substitute for quiet consideration'.

What with the trip into the desert, and the subsequent inspection of the storage shed at the docks, I was no longer band-box fresh. A trip to Parkside was indicated. I would take a shower and grab a clean shirt before embarking on the evening shift. Outside, the heat was gone from the sun, but there was plenty stored up in buildings and pavements, and the air in the city was breathless. There wasn't too much traffic at that hour, and I pointed thankfully homeward. A few blocks from Parkside I waited at a crossing, and realised that I was only a few hundred yards away from the Coffee Shop, the place where Rachel Steiner had reported seeing Suzanne Palmer. I made a left, and pulled in outside, looking the place over. I knew it by reputation only, and what I heard was good. It was known for good food, excellent service and roomy tables. There were no gimmicks, not even music, and it had a good, steady clientele who seemed to be able to afford the prices. If Suzanne wanted to keep out of the public eye, she'd picked a good place to work in. It drew its customers from the upper income brackets, but it wasn't the prices which kept out the undesirables. Plenty of those in the high-roll category. What kept them away was the absence of anything they normally sought when they went out. No band, no oily emcee to call out their names, no one who cared about their presence at all. For people to whom recognition is the essence of life, places like the Coffee Shop represent some kind of instant death.

I was going to have to proceed with care when I got inside. The management would not take kindly to someone like me, asking questions about one of the staff. If I didn't watch my step, I could cost the girl her job, and I hoped Shad Steiner knew how much trouble his little favour was liable to cause.

It was cool in there, and the

layout was much as I had imagined. Heavy mahogany furniture, and the general trappings of some baronial dining hall. Lights reflected softly from gleaming wood and polished silver. The glassware, you knew, would be crystal.

"Good evening sir."

At this a man in a full tail suit looked at me enquiringly.

"Evening," I returned, conscious that I lacked that clean shirt.

"Is the manager around?"

"Please follow me."

There were a few early diners putting the silver to good use, and appetising smells drifted maddeningly across the path as I walked through the dining room to a small door. The absence of any kind of bar was noticeable.

"I'll just see if he's free."

My guide disappeared inside, and I stood there feeling conspicuous. Not that anybody was interested. They were far too concerned with the contents of their plates After a moment the door opened again, and thin-face waved me inside.

"You wished to see me? I am Hamilton Parkes, the manager."

He didn't get up from his desk, and there was no handshake. He was smooth-faced and round, with fair hair and pale eyes, about forty five years old. We looked each other over, and he decided he had the better of the inspection. I'd already reached the same conclusion.

"The name is Preston. I'm a private investigator."

To save him asking for identification, I held it out for inspection. He studied it keenly, then nodded.

"What can I do for you, Mr Preston?"

"I'm trying to trace a young woman. Some friends are worried about her, because she hasn't been in touch for some time. I believe she may be working here. Her name is Suzanne Palmer."

There was no reaction on his face.

"Palmer? No, I'm afraid you have been misinformed, Mr Preston. There is no one on the staff by that name."

He waited for me to leave. Instead, I pulled out the photograph.

"She could have changed her name. There is no law against it."

This time he showed more interest, leaning forward and peering at the picture in my hand intently.

"Yes," he confirmed, "that is Susan Follet. She works here. A most pleasant and capable young woman. I don't very much care for this, Mr Preston. This is not the kind of establishment where we can tolerate people using assumed names."

If I didn't tread carefully, I was going to cost the girl her job.

"I doubt whether that's the situation," I soothed. "Palmer was her married name, you see. Her husband died in an accident. She's probably reverted to her maiden name."

"I shall most certainly ask her, when she returns," he assured me.

"Returns? You mean she's away?"

"She called in sick today. Most inconvenient, and such short notice. Not like her at all."

It was evident that in Hamilton Parkes book, people falling sick should give seven days notice of their intention.

"That's too bad. I want to have a word with her. Do you have an address where I might contact her?"

For the first time, there was animation on his face.

"An address? Certainly, I have an address. As for giving it to you Mr Preston, the answer is no. Staff records are confidential. I've no doubt Miss Follet will be back to work in a day or two. You will have to wait. And now, if there's nothing further — ?"

There was nothing further. This wasn't a man I could push too hard without making him suspicious.

"Well, thanks for the cooperation, Mr Parkes. I'll probably look around tomorrow, to see if the lady's reported."

He considered this for a moment.

"I can't prevent you from doing that, of course. However, I trust you will not distress her on the premises. The essence of our atmosphere here is dignity. Dignity and calm."

If I read him right, I could distress her as much as I pleased, off the premises.

"I'll be the soul of discretion," I assured him, and he nodded, pushing a button on the desk.

The head waiter appeared. He must have been hovering outside the whole time.

"George," announced Parkes, "this is Mr Preston. As you know, I shall be away most of tomorrow. Mr Preston wishes to talk with our Miss Follet on a little family matter. It will be in order for them to use my office for the purpose."

He wasn't doing me any favour. What he meant was, if I was going to upset the girl, I could do it where the customers didn't have to watch. Dignity being the essence, and all.

"Thanks again Mr Parkes. Good-night."

I followed George outside. He was working his tongue around inside his mouth, as though trying to dig some words out of his teeth. When we reached the entrance he blurted out.

"Mr Preston, I know who you are. I've seen your picture in the papers. Is Susan in some kind of trouble?"

"Not that I know of," I said carefully. "Why should you think that?"

He glanced nervously over his shoulder, as though expecting his boss to appear.

"Because you're the second person here today, asking about her," he replied.

It began to look as though Shad Steiner's favour might be going to pay off.

"Tell me what happened. Please," I added, "all I want is to help the girl. Who else was asking about her?"

"I didn't see him myself. He talked to one of our other girls, Laurie Winters.

She'd better tell you herself. If you go around to the rear, I'll send her out to you."

He seemed genuine enough, but I worry a lot.

"Why are you doing this, George?"

Again that checking back, for signs of Parkes.

"I like the kid," he told me frankly, "and I didn't like the sound of what Laurie told me. Susan doesn't have anyone to look out for her, and this other man could mean trouble. Talk to Laurie."

I fished in my pocket for money, and his face went stony, as he sensed what I was about to do. Luckily, I caught the expression in time, and left my hand where it was.

"Thanks a lot, George. I'll be waiting."

Outside, I cut through an alleyway between the buildings, and found my way to the rear entrance of the Coffee Shop. I'd barely made it when the steel exit door swung open, and a tall dark-haired girl stepped out. I went over to her.

"Miss Winters?"

"Mrs," she corrected. "Just call me Laurie. George says you want to talk to me about Susan."

"Right," I nodded. "Cigaret?"

She hesitated, but not for long.

"That's the only problem with this job," she confided. "No smoking, and brother they mean no smoking. Old Favorites, huh? Wish I could afford these. George says it's O.K. to talk to you Mr Preston, so go ahead with your questions."

"It's very important that I get in touch with Susan as soon as possible," I assured her seriously. "And I don't like the idea that someone else wants her. Would you tell me what happened, Laurie?"

She inhaled smoke with evident satisfaction.

"There was this man, he came in around two o'clock today. He ordered some lunch, but he didn't really eat it. Asked me where Susan was, and I told him she was sick. Then he asked if I knew where she lived. Said he was a friend of the family, just in town for one day from the east, and he wouldn't want to go back without seeing her. I told him I didn't know her address, but he could probably get it from Mr Parkes. He said he'd do that, and I got on with my work. Next thing I knew, he'd left. And," she added with heavy emphasis, "he didn't go near Mr Parkes. I knew he was a phoney."

"What made you suspect him?"

"He got her name wrong, for one thing. Called her Suzanne. You'd think a friend of the family would know a girl's name. Besides that, I been waiting on tables for ten years, all round here. I know a native Californian when I see one. What's this all about, Mr Preston?"

"I don't know yet," I answered, with perfect truth. "But I think your friend could be in some kind of danger. Tell me more about this man. What did he look like?"

She looked up at the sky while thinking. Laurie Winters must have been a pretty girl when she started out, but she had one of those round faces which can sag early if the owner isn't careful. Already, a second chin was making growing noises.

"I didn't get to see him standing up," she reminded me, "but I'd guess he was your height. Sandy hair, close crop, and a very lean face, kind of like an Indian, you know? Casual clothes, but they were expensive. I'd say he was late twenties. Very strong hands, I noticed."

"That's a very good description, Laurie," I flattered. "You'd have made a detective I should imagine. And you certainly did Susan a favour, not telling that man where to find her. You do know the address, don't you?"

"Oh sure, I know it. I gave her a lift there one time, when her car was being fixed. How do I know I can trust you, Mr Preston?"

"Because you know who I am," I replied easily. "So does George, don't forget. If I did Susan any harm, I couldn't get away with it, because you people could identify me. Besides, all you'll be doing is beating the clock. I can see her here tomorrow, just by walking in. This other man can do the same thing, remember. Don't you think it's better if I see her first?"

It was an appeal to her own judgement, always a tough one to resist.

"I guess that's right enough," she assented, frowning. "You won't tell Mr Parkes you got it from me?"

"Absolutely not," I promised.

"She's at 4040 Chilton. Fifth floor. I forget the number."

"I'll find it. Thanks a lot, Laurie, and I'm sure you're doing Susan a favour."

Again, I had that problem about whether or not to slip her a few bills for her trouble, and again I sensed that I might be going to make a mistake. An idea struck me, and I held out the near-full pack of Old Favorites.

"Here," I said, thrusting them out. "I was about to quit smoking anyway. These might as well go to a good home."

She hesitated, then took them.

"Tell her I hope she's better soon."

"Will do."

I went back to the car. The late sun was showing some red as it sank towards the ocean, and I had a vague recollection that was either very good news for the shepherds, or very bad. Let them tend their own flocks, anyway. There was only one lost sheep I was concerned with, and I set out to track her down.

7

4040 Chilton was a medium rental apartment block which narrowly justified inclusion in the Heights postal district. For a girl whose only known source of income was that of a waitress in a high-class restaurant, Suzanne Palmer was living well. All the parking slots were occupied, and I settled for a spot almost opposite the building on the other side of the street. As I climbed out, a car backed away from a space outside the entrance, and I hesitated about whether to take its place. The decision was made for me by a blue Packard which rounded the corner at that moment and slid smoothly into the new space. The world is divided into two classes of people. Those who can never find anywhere to park, and opportunists in blue Packards. I made my way across the wide thoroughfare, collecting two horn-blasts and one waved fist en route. Then I went into the building. I'd been hoping there might be a list of occupants in the vestibule, but that was a service not provided by the management. It was a relief to discover that the elevator worked, and I emerged at five to find myself in the usual corridor, with doors heading away in both directions. I decided to try the left side first, and scanned the nameplates as I went along. There was only the corner unit left, Number 501, — and I was relieved to see one word typed on the small white card. Follet.

I pressed the buzzer and stood well clear, so that I could be easily inspected through the spy-hole. There was no response, and I repeated the performance. There was no sound up there, and I was straining my ears for signs of movement inside the apartment. Finally I thought I heard faint indications from behind the door, but there was still no reply. This time I leaned on the bell-push for a whole ten seconds, making it clear that I wasn't about to go away.

"Who is it?"

A woman's voice came faintly through.

"Police," I announced. "Open up."

"Have you any authority?" she asked querulously.

I opened up my leather. Years before, I'd been made a deputy sheriff of Wahoo County or someplace. It wasn't much more than a gag at the time, but the sticker impresses people who don't know any better. After a pause, there was a general sliding and rattling noise, and the door swung open. The woman who stood there wasn't looking her best, but there was no mistaking that she was the one in the photograph Steiner had given me.

"You'd better come in," she said resignedly.

We went in to the comfortable apartment. On a side table, I noticed a bottle of tequila which had been getting plenty of action. A half-empty glass rested on a coffee-table, next to an ashtray containing a smouldering cigaret. Suzanne Palmer ground out the butt with quick nervous movements, and promptly lit another. Her good-looking face was strained, and her hair hadn't had much attention today. I remembered she was supposed to be sick, but I would have thought her condition was due more to worry than to anything medical. I certainly hoped so.

"I imagine you know why I'm here," I bluffed.

She nodded unhappily.

"It's about poor Mr Hadley, isn't it? I guess I should have come to you right off."

"You should," I confirmed briskly. "You have some explaining to do, Mrs Palmer. Mind if I sit down?"

She waved a vague hand, and I parked on a comfortable upright. A nervous puff at the cigarette, and she sat herself abruptly down opposite, not looking at me.

"I'm waiting," I reminded her.

"What is it you want to know?"

This was the hard part. If I gave her the slightest impression that I didn't know which way was up, she would smell a rat, and I'd be it. Fortunately for me, she wasn't the hard-bitten kind, who'd shout about lawyers and warrants. She was just a frightened girl, who was close to the end of her tether, and if I handled her right, I was about to learn something.

"All of it," I snapped. "From the top. And don't leave anything out, Mrs Palmer. It hasn't been easy tracking you down, and I've wasted enough time."

Now, she picked up the glass and swallowed some of the pale spirit.

"I'm glad you found me," she announced, "before they did."

This was what I'd come for. So there was a 'they'. And no doubt one of them was a sandy-haired man with a lean face.

"They won't be far behind," I said

solemnly. "One of them was at the Coffee Shop today, asking about you. He talked to Laurie Winters, but she was suspicious of him, and wouldn't tell him where you lived. You have a good friend there."

That brought a faint smile to the tight features.

"Bless her for that. Where shall I start? There's so much — !"

"Go right back to the beginning," I suggested. "We know most of it, but there are gaps here and there."

"Right back to Larry?"

"Especially Larry," I confirmed.

"Poor Larry." She lifted the glass again, and this time it was empty when it hit the table. "If he hadn't had that terrible accident, we might have been rich by now. I suppose you know about that."

It was maddening, the way she kept passing the ball back.

"We haven't heard your side of the story."

"No. Well, Larry had this job out

159

at Ag-Mach. One day he came home, and he was all excited. We were about to get our big break, he told me, and we'd be on easy street in no time."

"What was this big break?" I probed.

She shook her head, and I didn't feel she was being evasive.

"I never really understood it. Larry was on the design side, you know, and I think he was good at his job. Anyway, he'd made some kind of break-through, something technical. He didn't bother to try explaining it to me, because he knew I probably wouldn't understand anyway. When it comes to engineering, I'm the original fluff."

A technical break-through. I began to feel the way the old miners must have felt when they first saw the signs of pay-dirt. I don't know engineering either, but I know a hole when I see one.

"Who else was involved at the plant? Did he mention any names?"

"Not at the time. I didn't ask a lot of questions about it. As I say, the answer would have meant nothing to me, anyway. Then, after he — after he was killed, Mr Hadley came to see me. He was very nice, very sympathetic. He wanted to know how much Larry had confided in me, and I told him what I'm telling you. That was when he advised me to move away."

That might have made sense to her, but I couldn't follow it.

"Why did he suggest that?"

"He told me that other people were after this new design that Larry had invented. The details weren't perfect yet, and the big companies wanted to get hold of the patent. They'd stop at nothing, he told me, and they certainly wouldn't spare me, just because I'm a woman. As Larry's widow, you see, I had the right to file those papers in my own name. Mr Hadley wanted to help me to do that, but I'd have to get away somewhere safe in the meantime. So I moved, night after the funeral, and I didn't tell anybody where I was going."

"Except Hadley," I pointed out.

"Except him, naturally. He helped me find this place."

I looked around the apartment, and wondered again how she could afford it.

"Kind of expensive, isn't it?" I asked, trying to sound casual.

"Yes, it is," she agreed. "I could never have run to it, but he told me not to worry about that. He paid he the rent, three months ahead, and the deposit, too. He said I could call it a kind of loan. I could pay him back later, when the Patent office had issued the papers. I'd be rich then, he told me. But now — "

Her face was beginning to crumple, and evidently the support she'd been getting from the tequila was beginning to wear off. Making my tone as conciliatory as I could, bearing in mind that I was supposed to be a police officer, I said.

"Mrs Palmer, why don't you go and make us both some coffee? You look as if you could do with it, and I could use a cup."

Almost like a child, who was grateful to be given clear instructions, she got up and went out of the room. I lit an Old Favorite, and thought over what she'd been telling me.

The part about her late husband and his design I could believe. It was entirely consistent with what I already knew. Larry Palmer had either created something, or stumbled across something, and there was big money at the end of it. He then died, either as the result of an accident, or because he was becoming a nuisance to some third party. O.K. So far. Next, Hadley appeared, and that was a development that didn't fit. I'm nobody's business efficiency expert, but even I knew that a draughtsman doesn't work for an accountant. Palmer should have been with Sturges, or a production engineer, someone on the technical side of the company. Then there was the way Hadley simply took over when

163

the husband died. I could see where that wouldn't have been too difficult for him. Suzanne Palmer wasn't up there with the leaders in the I.Q. race for one thing. She'd listen to a smooth character like Hadley, and, with not too much money around, she'd be ripe for any positive line of action suggested, particularly from somebody of Hadley's status in the company. As for the yarn about the big industrialists wanting to get their hands on the secret, whatever it was, that was a staple of a large percentage of the tee-vee programs. It wouldn't be too difficult to sell a story like that to somebody gullible, especially if the mark was newly bereaved.

No. I could understand how Hadley would have been able to do it.

The point was, why?

Why would he take it on himself to spirit the girl away? She had no knowledge of what her husband had been doing. She was no threat to anybody. And why would he spread cash to pay rent on her new apartment? What was supposed to happen at the end of the three months rental? It could be that he was just being Mr Nice Guy, but I dismissed the possibility. There's nice and nice. Nice does not usually include promoting all that hard cash out of a man's own pocket. Two other possibilities suggested themselves. One was that Suzanne somehow presented a threat to Hadley, and he wanted her out of the way while he decided what was to be done about her. The other was that she was his insurance, his ace-in-the-hole. If Palmer's death had not been the accident it seemed, then someone had killed him. It was just possible that Hadley felt his own life was at risk, and was using Suzanne in some way as his guarantee that they couldn't harm him. He could have told those people, whoever they were, that she knew the whole story, and if anything should happen to him, she would go to the authorities. The well-known mystery witness angle.

The most obvious explanation of all was that there was something between them, and I was now sitting in the love-nest, but I didn't buy that. The man had been too concerned about what his own wife was up to. If he'd been playing footsie with Suzanne Palmer, he'd have been only too pleased to let his wife get on with whatever she was doing, so long as she kept out of his hair. In those circumstances, a man does not hire an expensive investigator to find out what's going on. The feel of it was wrong. Besides which, there was the hard fact of Dexter Hadley's murder. More than one person had been involved in that, which implied some kind of organisation.

All this speculation was still whirling inconclusively around in my head when the lady hostess came back with the coffee. Wordlessly, she passed a cup to me, and I set it down in front of me.

"Mrs Palmer, if I'm to believe what you're telling me, we could have a big lead about Mr Hadley's death. Did he ever give you any indication of who these people might be? Did he mention any names, did you ever see any of them?"

She pulled away a strand of hair which had fallen over her eyes.

"No. All I know is what he told me. They were powerful people, who would stop at nothing. That's what he said. Well, he was right, wasn't he? They've killed him, and now they're looking for me."

Her hands began to shake, and some of the coffee slopped into the saucer as she raised the cup to her lips. If I didn't handle her with care, she was going to dissolve on me.

"Tell me, do you have any papers here belonging to your late husband? Or anything you were keeping for Mr Hadley?"

"No," she refuted, "nothing like that. There were some drawings, stuff that Larry used to work on at home, but Mr Hadley took those away, soon after Larry — after Larry — "

A tremor came into her voice, and the words tailed away.

Hadley seemed to have thought of everything, I reflected savagely.

"You're certain about that?" I pressed. "No old notebooks, or anything that might give us a lead?"

"Nothing. He even took the books, said he'd like to have them if I didn't mind. After all he'd done for me, it was the least I could do. Besides, I didn't have any use for them. Made me think of Larry every time I looked at them."

The books. I seized at the straw as it floated through the conversation.

"What books are we talking about?" I asked, trying to sound casual.

"Oh, all that war stuff, you know. Poor Larry was always studying up on all the wars. Not just Nam and Korea, but way back to World War One."

A war buff. It sounded like a dead end. If some body started bumping off everybody who wanted to play soldiers, the streets would be littered.

On the other hand, why would Hadley want them? It seemed to be stretching coincidence a little far, to assume that he was also an amateur military historian.

"Do you happen to recall any of the titles?"

She shook her head.

"They all sounded the same to me. Just boring. I have the list though, if you'd like to see it."

"It probably won't help, but I'd better take a look."

She went away again, and I tested the coffee. Terrible. You'd think somebody who worked in a place called the Coffee Shop would at least learn the technique.

"Here it is. I came across it the other day. I would have thrown it away, but it's in his own hand writing, and it would have been like tossing out a piece of him. Does that sound foolish?"

"No," I assured her gently. "It sounds very normal to me."

It wasn't a very long list, eighteen or twenty titles. Larry Palmer's handwriting was very square and clear, the kind one would expect from a man who was accustomed to setting out explanatory notes on his drawings. I glanced at the titles without much hope.

'Advances in Military Technology.'

'Warplanes of the Past.'

etc. etc.

It was evident that Palmer's interest was not the kind where people re-fight the great battles, or study the military tactics. His concern was with the hardware. I handed the paper back to Suzanne.

"Not much there to help us, I'm afraid. Tell me though, just out of interest, if your late husband was so interested in the military area, why didn't he get a job with one of the government agencies, or an aircraft company? He could have been paid for working on his hobby. A lot of people would be glad of the chance."

"He talked about it sometimes," she nodded. "But it always came back to the same thing. He could see himself being stuck in a corner, and working on something that didn't interest him at all, or something he could see was going to be useless in the end. He always used to say those places didn't want people with real ideas. They had the ideas, or thought they had. All they needed was hacks, to put them down on paper. There was another big objection he had, too, although I used to think he was kidding himself, to tell you the truth."

I really didn't want to get stuck in all this family history, but it wouldn't have paid to discourage her from talking.

"What might that have been?"

"He always used to say that if he came up with some new idea, some big break-through, he wouldn't get the credit for it. They would say it was all part of the job, and he wouldn't even be able to register the patent."

There was an element of truth in

that. I'd heard odd complaints about similar situations from time to time.

"And was he interested in that side of it?" I asked. "I mean, new designs and so on."

"Heavens yes. That's what all the drawings were about," she exclaimed, sounding almost surprised that I hadn't realised that earlier. "He was always working on some new airplane, or tank, or missile. One time, there was this new kind of submarine. That was the cause of our first big quarrel. He'd stayed up half the night working on it, and I told him enough was enough."

She smiled reminiscently, then two large tears welled suddenly up in the luminous eyes, and rolled unheeded down her cheeks. Until that moment, she had been coming slowly back to normal, and this was no time for her to crumple. I said sharply.

"Mrs Palmer, I think you're probably in danger from those other people, whoever they are. Do you have any-where you could go for a few days? A friend, a relative?"

The change in subject, and in my tone, brought a look of shocked surprise to her face.

"Danger? But not now you're here? You'll protect me."

Her voice was more like that of a child, an appeal to the trusted adult to take care of everything. It was with real reluctance that I shook my head.

"I'd help you if I could, but I'm in no position. You see, I'm not with the regular force. I'm just a State licensed investigator, and I don't have any back-up facilities."

Trust gave way to alarm.

"But you could tell them. You could tell the real police — "

She broke off, at the decisive shaking of my head.

"Tell them what? It's all so vague. Who would want to hurt you, and why? You can't produce any reasons, much less names, and neither can I. The police would be very interested to talk with you, its true, but they don't have the manpower to guard anyone who may or may not be in danger. Go to them, by all means. Tell them what you know. But take my advice. Have a bag with you, and don't come back here. Go straight to your friends, and stay there. I don't understand any of this, any more than you do. But we both know what happened to Hadley. People who will do a thing like that won't hesitate to do it again." I got up to leave. "I can't force you, Mrs Palmer, but remember this. I found you. If I did it, others can do it. It's up to you. Thanks for the coffee."

She was watching me nervously, unsure as to whether I might attack her, even then. I smiled re-assuringly and walked to the door. She came scurrying after me.

"Wait," she begged, "I haven't even thanked you."

"It isn't necessary. The best thanks you can give me is to follow my advice and get away from here." Then a thought struck me. "I'll tell you what.

If you feel like contacting my office some time, just call the number on this card. You don't have to say where you are, only that you're all right. I'd feel easier, if I knew that."

She took the card, nodding, and pressed my arm. The tears were not far away again, and I am no great shakes as a comforter. I left her in the tiny hallway, and went out. On the way downstairs I had a feeling that I might have learned something from Suzanne Palmer, but I couldn't isolate what it was. All that chatter about submarines. Was it possible that her husband had really come up with something new in that direction?

It seemed unlikely.

In any case, even if he had, it was a long way moved from an AG4B earth-mover. You didn't have to drill holes in one of those to make it sink. Anything less seaworthy than one of the great ungainly machines would be hard to visualise. No, it couldn't have been that. What then?

I was still puzzling over every little thing she said when I got into the car, and started the motor. I had to back out into traffic, and kept a watchful eye on the rear view mirror. As I swung into position, I had a clear view of the entrance to Suzanne's apartment block. A man climbed out of the blue Packard and straightened up. He was a tall man.

With sandy hair.

8

HE stood there for a moment, watching me leave. I made a left, to the annoyance of a truck driver who wasn't expecting it, and pulled in around the corner. Then I jumped out, and went back down the street fast. There was no sign of the tall man. Inside the building, the elevator lights were flashing rapidly upwards. There was a bank of three, and I jumped into the next one, pressing the button marked 'Four'. If the sandy man was who I thought he might be, he'd check automatically on the other elevators when he reached the fifth floor. When he saw the lights stop at four, he'd lose interest, and get on with what he came for. The numbers on the panel climbed upwards with maddening slowness. Surely the thing had been faster than this last time?

Finally I reached four and rushed out, looking for the stairs. Up I went, two at a time, and panting with exertion when I got to the top. The sandy man had a start on me, of maybe twenty seconds, and a lot can happen in that time. Carefully, I edged the wooden door open, and stared out into the corridor, easing the thirty eight into my hand. If the visitor had any connection with the deaths of Palmer and Hadley, he wasn't calling on the widow to offer his condolences.

He said something to the door, but I couldn't catch the words. Then he spoke again. This time, his hand disappeared inside the alpaca jacket and came out holding a heavy calibre automatic. I pushed open my door and stepped out.

"Hey," I called.

He turned, startled, towards the new voice and I had the advantage by about two seconds. I fired, aiming for the shoulder, and his gun went off at almost the same time. My bullet struck him just in time to deflect his aim, and lead spanged into the wall at my left. Then he lost his hold on the gun, as he grabbed his upper arm in pain. I went forward quickly, kicking the weapon out of his reach, and bending down to pick it up.

He glared at me in a mixture of rage and surprise. There was no trace of fear.

"You're a dead man," he gritted.

I was opposite the apartment door now, and Suzanne must have seen me through the spyhole, because it swung open. She stood there, white-faced, taking in the scene. For a moment, I was afraid she might throw a screaming fit, but she was oddly calm, looking at me with questioning eyes.

"We're coming in," I told her, "don't get anywhere near this animal."

She almost jumped back, in her anxiety to follow instructions. I waggled the automatic, for our new friend to step inside. He made no move, but simply stood there, clutching his ruined arm. Blood was beginning to seep between his fingers.

"Your choice," I assured him. "Either you go inside, or I finish you now, and dump you in the elevator."

To give emphasis to the threat, I banged at his wound with the heavy metal, forcing a grunt of startled pain from his tight lips. For the first time there was something besides annoyance in his eyes. He turned and walked in to the apartment, Suzanne pressing herself flat against the wall as he walked past.

"Get the door locked," I instructed.

She hastened to obey, and fell in behind our little procession. When we were in the living room, the sandy-haired man paused, and turned round.

"Now what?" he demanded.

"The shoes. Take 'em off," I commanded. "You can either do it yourself, or I'll do it my way."

A slight movement of the thirty-eight was sufficient to persuade him which method he preferred. Levering awkwardly with his feet he eased off first one shoe then the other.

"You oughtn't to wear blue socks with brown slacks," I tutted. "Shame on you. Suzanne, do you have a waste-disposal?"

"Why yes."

"Put the shoes down it," I instructed.

"I tell you Preston, you're dead," repeated the sandy-haired man.

"Wrong," I corrected. "You're much closer to it than me, and I'm the one with the gun. Take off your coat."

But the use of my name was a cause for concern. He knew who I was, and where there was one there would be others. Suzanne came back from getting rid of the shoes, and stood looking at us each in turn. Sandy was wincing and grunting as he tried to take off his jacket without giving himself too much pain.

"Do you know him?" I asked.

"No," she denied. "I've never seen him before. Why did you — I mean, did you have to — "

"Shoot him?" I finished. "Yes, I did.

It was either him or you. What was it he said to you?"

"I don't know. I really don't know. He was saying something but it wasn't much above a whisper. I couldn't catch the words."

I nodded, satisfied.

"You weren't intended to," I explained. "You knew he was talking to you, and you got up close to the door, trying to hear the words, right?"

"Why yes," she confirmed, still not understanding.

I was still holding his automatic, a four-four Colt.

"He was going to kill you, through the door," I told her. "This thing would have gone through that wood as if it were paper. I had to stop him, and there wasn't time for a chat. Naughty."

The last word was addressed to Sandy. He'd got the coat free, and was swinging it towards my gun hand. Side-stepping easily, I watched it sail harmlessly by, then I went over and stamped on one blue-socked foot.

"Why don't you be nice?" I advised.

His face was working with pain and frustrated rage, but I had to give him credit. He showed no signs of folding up. I scooped up the jacket, passing the automatic for Suzanne to hold.

"Do you understand these things?" I queried.

She handled it knowingly, and nodded.

"Oh yes," she confided. "Larry made me take a course in pistol-shooting. He used to say every woman ought to be able to defend herself."

Good for Larry, I reflected.

"Fine. Stand over there by the window. If this imitation Al Capone moves one finger, shoot him. Try not to kill him, if you can help it, but shoot him anyway."

"Why don't we put him on a chair?" she suggested. "That way, he'd have to get up before he could start anything."

I looked at her with new respect. Plenty of females would have been yowling in a corner, an extra liability.

Suzanne Palmer was not merely holding up one end, she was making a contribution.

"Good," I concurred.

She fetched an upright chair from another room, and dumped it down beside the watching Sandy. He wasn't missing a move, and his eyes had widened slightly at the practised way in which she had held the automatic. With him on the chair, and Suzanne over by the window, plus gun, I felt able to give my attention to the coat. There were some keys, which I transferred to my own pocket, then some bills, eighteen dollars in all, which I left. Next came a driver's license, in the name of Peter Kowalski. Tucked inside was a business card. This informed the reader that Mr Kowalski was a representative for the Monkton Export Company, with a regular business address and telephone number. It was that word 'export' which filled my mind with beautiful thoughts.

"There was a Kowalski used to play

left field for the Buffaloes," I said conversationally. "That wasn't you, was it?"

He said nothing, but stared grimly at the floor. He'd lost a fair amount of blood from the bullet-wound, but that had ceased flowing now, leaving him only with the throbbing pain.

"Pete, you are going to have to talk to me, so why don't we just start? Who sent you here?"

"Why don't you just go to hell?" he suggested. "I got nothing to say to you. I don't talk to dead people. It's kinky."

I had met too many characters like him in the past to delude myself that I could persuade him to talk. He was more afraid of the people who employed him than of me or the police. There was just one area where I might find a way through.

"You're going to need a doctor for that arm," I began.

"There'll be one," he stated flatly. "You can't keep me here for ever. And don't waste my time with talk about killing me and stuff. That's for birds. You ain't gonna kill nobody. Neither is your girl-friend."

I listened to this carefully, and nodded.

"That's true," I conceded, "as far as it goes. Only thing is, if you don't get that arm fixed, and quick, I might have killed you already."

Kowalski wasn't the brightest of people, and I could almost trace the thoughts, chasing each other across his forehead, as he tried to puzzle that one out.

"I don't get it," he said finally. "A slug in the arm? When was the last time somebody died from a slug in the arm?"

"This particular slug is different," I explained. "You see, when I load the piece, I always rub each cartridge with garlic. Do I need to tell you what that means? It's an old Sicilian trick, Pete. The wound goes septic, then it turns to gangrene. It's no problem to a doctor, if he catches if fast enough. But, once the wound is a couple of hours old, there's nothing they can do. They'll try, naturally. They'll amputate, see if that works, but you have no more than a fifty-fifty chance. You're right, I'm not going to kill you. I don't have to. We'll just sit around a couple of hours, then you can go."

Some of the color went out of his face.

"You're bluffing," he snarled.

"O.K." I returned cheerfully. "Suzanne, why don't you fix us a drink? We're going to be here some time, might as well be comfortable."

There was something akin to horror on her face, but I could do nothing about that. I couldn't tell her the whole thing was a fabrication, and on two counts. In the first place, there wasn't any garlic, but that wasn't the largest part of the bluff. The whole thing is a myth, anyway. There's no scientific foundation for the ancient belief but it holds its ground among the curious lore of the criminal fraternity. The thin line of sweat which began to form on Kowalski's upper lip told me more than any of his words.

Suzanne shook her head, as if that might dislodge the horror of what I'd done to the man in the chair. The fact that he could have killed her ten minutes earlier seemed already to have faded from her memory.

"We have to get this man to a hospital," she urged.

He looked at her with quick hope, but I only sighed.

"Right," I agreed. "That's what we have to do. That's what we will do, two hours from now. How about that drink?"

"It's murder," she blurted.

"Wrong," I corrected. "It's suicide. He can be at hospital in ten minutes. All he has to do is to tell me what I want to know. Don't blame me, lady."

She made an impatient tutting noise, and relapsed into a resentful silence.

Kowalski, realising that the subject was closed, stared at the floor again. I lit an Old Favorite. Evidently, I wasn't going to get my drink, and the wounded man was not so helpless that I was prepared to get it myself turning my back on him in the process.

"Do they have a pension fund over at Monkton Export?" I asked conversationally. "You know, with a regular death benefit and so forth?"

He glowered at me, and now his whole face was beginning to shine, as the fear sweated its way through.

"What will you take to let me go?" he demanded. "You want money? I can get it. Listen — "

I yawned.

"Money? What use is that to me if I'm dead? No, Pete, you're going to have to do better than money. I need information."

He swore, and made to raise his arm towards me, but the sudden movement jarred the wound, and he let out a long sigh of pain as fresh blood appeared.

"I don't know anything," he protested feebly.

"Oh, tut tut," I reproved. "You're too modest by half. You knew enough to track down this lady to where she worked. You knew I was involved, and if you followed me around, I might lead you to her. You knew somebody wanted her dead, and you were prepared to do that little chore. I'd say you know all kinds of stuff, Pete. Why don't you spread some of it around? You already wasted nearly fifteen minutes, by the way. Is it beginning to throb? That's the way it usually starts."

That's the way any bullet wound starts, so it was a safe question.

"Go to hell," he suggested.

I laughed.

"You'll be there before me," I promised. "Crazy thing about this is, you don't need to die at all. You'll tell everything you know, once the infection spreads. That's one of the things that happens. People start to hallucinate, and they just talk their heads off. Either you can talk to me now, and stay alive, or I can wait. You'll talk to me later, you'll talk to the whole world later. And then you'll die. I only ever saw it happen once, but its not something a man forgets. So go ahead. Be a hero. Time means nothing to me."

Suzanne opened her mouth as if to protest again, but I silenced her with a withering stare. Kowalski licked at the sweat which was running down his lip.

"You swear you'll take me to proper hospital?"

"Monkton General is just a few blocks away. A matter of minutes."

"If I talk, they'll kill me," he muttered.

"Perhaps," I agreed. "But they have to get to you first. Once you get that arm fixed, you could be out of town long before they even know anything happened. It won't be a joyride, but it beats what'll happen to you otherwise."

He nodded, as though coming to terms with himself.

"I don't know much," he hedged, "not the real important stuff."

"I'll be the judge of that. Who's the top man?"

The look of horror on his face was not assumed.

"Top man? You crazy or something? Guys like me don't get near those kind of people. I wouldn't know him if he walked in the door. I just do what I'm told."

"And who tells you?" I pressed.

He hesitated, then narrowed his eyes, and the decision was made.

"Tom Brewer, he's the boss."

I ran the name around the memory banks inside my head, but it came up blank.

"Where do I find him?"

"Where it tells you on the card. Tom is like the manager of the company."

I looked again at the business card I'd removed from his pocket.

"Monkton Exports?" I queried, and he nodded. "But this is a regular business address."

"Why not?" he countered. "It's a regular business."

"Not many regular businesses employ people like you, Pete. No offense, but you have to admit it's kind of unusual."

He stuck out his lower lip.

"I ain't exactly on the regular payroll. I just do like what you might call piecework. When they need something doing, Tom calls me up and puts me to work. They get some funny customers, you know?"

"No, I don't know," I looked at my watch. "Look Pete, I don't want to hurry you, but twenty minutes have gone. What kind of business are they in, where they need you to deal with the customers?"

He looked at me oddly, then at Suzanne.

"If you don't know nothing, why do they want her dead?" he asked cunningly. "Seems an awful waste of a nice-looking dame."

"If I knew that," I assured him, "I

wouldn't be wasting time talking to you. I'll ask you again. What business are these people in? What is it that gets exported?"

"Everything," and again he tried to shrug. "Rifles, pistols, grenades, dynamite, ammunition — "

"Armaments?" I repeated unnecessarily.

"I'm telling you, ain't I? Sure armaments, what else? It don't go out that way, natch. It goes out like farm machinery, tools, medical supplies, you name it. Listen, that's all there is. How about this hospital?"

He wasn't exactly whining but there was a note of increasing urgency in his voice. Suzanne too, was fidgeting, and I felt I wouldn't be able to control the charade for much longer.

I shook my head.

"Not yet. I'm not satisfied Pete. I need more. This yakety about people running guns, I don't buy that. It's all too big-time for you, or for me. What I'm dealing with here is a simple murder. A guy gets killed, I want to know who killed him, that's all. I don't need all these movie scripts."

He looked imploringly at Suzanne, and his face was working.

"Lady, I swear to God, that's all there is. Don't let him do this to me. You know what gangrene is?"

He spoke the last words on a high rising note, and the girl bit her lip.

"Mr Preston — " she began, tremulously.

"Mr Preston, nothing," I interrupted. "You have a short memory, Suzanne. It's only twenty minutes ago when this animal tried to kill you. Even if you choose to forget that you can't forget that he also killed your husband. If we hadn't been lucky, he'd have wiped out the whole family."

Her face hardened then, while she tried to absorb this new information.

"Larry?" she whispered. "What are you saying?"

It probably wasn't intentional, but her grip on the Colt tightened, and it was pointing at Kowalski. His anxious eyes did not miss the movement, and he must have decided she was about to kill him.

"That wasn't me," he blurted out, "I didn't do that. Tom did it, I swear to God, him and the woman."

Suzanne shook her head, as if to rid it of these new unwelcome thoughts.

"I don't understand," she muttered, and she wasn't speaking to either of us now.

"Leave this to me," I commanded. "Maybe he's telling the truth." Then, to the sweating man in the chair. "You can see how upset the lady is, Pete. You'd better give us the rest. What woman are you talking about?"

We weren't talking in abstracts now. We were talking about a murdered man, Larry Palmer, and the fact that his widow was holding a powerful handgun, which was pointed at his possible executioner. She could start squeezing that trigger at any moment, and Kowalski knew the face of death when he saw it.

"Don't know her name," he babbled. "I never saw her. But she's on the inside of all this. You'd have to get it from Tom. Tom Brewer, I told you about him. Listen, Preston, I swear to God — "

"Save it. How do you mean, she's on the inside? The inside of what?"

He rattled his head desperately.

"I don't know, for chrissakes. I'm just a guy with a gun. I do what they tell me. They tell me to take out this lady here, that's what I do. I don't know none of that stuff."

He was in a sufficient state of advanced terror now for me to believe him.

"You're saying she's Tom Brewer's woman then. Is that it?"

"No, no. That ain't what I'm saying. She's one of the people who tells Tom what to do, that's all. I don't know nothing about her, just she's a class lady, is all."

A class lady, I reflected. Oh sure. She would have to be a woman of some refinement, to get herself mixed up in illegal armaments and murder. Real high-toned. I ignored Kowalski for the moment, and spoke to Suzanne.

"Put the gun down, Suzanne," I instructed gently. "If it goes off, you could be killing the wrong man."

She looked over at me with pain and puzzlement on her face.

"Larry?" she implored. "Murdered?"

"I'm afraid so. But not by this man. We'll talk about it later. Right now, we have to get him to the hospital. That garlic is a killer, and we don't have too much time."

The reminder about the fictitious infection focussed both their attentions away from Larry Palmer's death. Suzanne rose obediently to her feet, awaiting the next move.

"Go and pack a bag," I instructed. "Take enough stuff to see you through three or four days at least. You won't be coming back here for a while."

She went away without another word, and the wounded man and I waited in silence, until she was ready. Then we all trooped down to my car, Kowalski still without shoes. Suzanne drove, and I sat in the rear with the patient. By this time, his whole attention was concentrated on the urgent need for medical care, and he was in no frame of mind to waste valuable time on escape attempts.

At the foot of the hospital steps, I handed him his coat. I'd replaced the wallet, with his identification inside, and the police would have no trouble in establishing who the gunshot victim was. I had toyed with the idea of putting the Colt in one of the pockets, but now had other plans for it. He scrambled out of the car, making one last show of defiance.

"Once I get out of here, I'll kill you," he promised.

"Ha ha," I replied. "I'll watch out for a man with one arm."

He clambered his painful way upwards, and I waved at Suzanne to drive away.

9

FIFTEEN minutes later, I was back at Parkside.

We had driven back to Suzanne Palmer's block, so that she could pick up her own car, then she had gone away to some friend's place, leaving me a telephone number. The sudden knowledge that Larry's death had been no accident had been a considerable shock to her, and she was going to need the next few days to adjust.

I called the Globe, and asked for Steiner. When the familiar gruntings sounded at the other end I said.

"Shad? This is an anonymous telephone call."

"The hell it is," he growled, "I'd know that voice anywhere."

"Listen," I urged, "either it's anonymous, or it stops now."

"I don't know what you're playing

at," he grumbled, "but O.K. What's it all about, Mr Whoever You Are?"

"I'm returning a favour," I announced loftily. "If you'd like to check your night mail box, you'll find a heavy brown envelope. There's a gun inside, a Colt four four. Handle with care, there are no prints on it."

A slight pause, then he said.

"What am I, an arms dealer?"

"It gets better," I assured him. "A man just arrived at Monkton Central with an unexplained gunshot wound. Who is this man, demands leading newspaper? Is there a connection between him and the automatic pistol left anonymously at these offices?"

"I don't know," he rejoined thoughtfully. "Is there? It would be hard to prove, with no prints on the gun."

"Tut tut Shad," I reproved. "No prints on the gun, true. But don't forget the cartridge clip. His prints will be all over that, you can bet."

"True," he agreed. "Would have been easier to leave 'em on the gun."

"Well," I explained, "that could have been embarrassing. The police might have found other prints. Prints of innocent parties."

"Ah," he sighed. "Even innocent anonymous parties?"

"It's possible," I agreed.

"Okay, so what have I got? A wounded man — you wouldn't be able to tell me how he got wounded, I imagine?"

"No, I don't have any information on that."

"I thought not. So, I have this wounded man, who may or may not connect with a certain pistol. So?"

"So, I think ballistics may find that weapon of interest," I suggested. "In fact, it would be no surprise to me if they decided it was one of the guns used to kill Dexter Hadley."

I waited then, to let that sink in.

"Do you now?" and he sounded more friendly. "Well, this begins to sound better. Why are you so good to me?"

"It's a trade," I explained. "I want the story to have good prominent coverage in the Globe. There are people around this town who think they're perfectly safe at the moment. The only little problem they might have is a certain private eye, and we both know who that is. If they see a big story in the Globe, they'll realise things are about to blow, and they might do something foolish. The least it will achieve is to make them nervous, and that can only be a plus."

"This investigator," he said, "you don't want him to have a little mention? A little free publicity?"

"He's a shy man," I assured him. "In fact, he's so shy, he would probably prefer it if you didn't mention him at all."

He chewed it over, but not for long. A man didn't hold down Steiner's job all those years without being able to make quick and sound decisions.

"You got it," he decided. "Hope you know what you're doing."

"Me too," I agreed. "When there's more, I'll get back to you."

"See you do," he grunted, and broke off.

I was thoughtful when I put down the telephone. Steiner had touched a sore spot when he said he hoped I knew what I was doing. It was only in the past hour that I'd begun to get a glimmering of what I was into. Up until then, I'd just been blundering around. If it hadn't been for Shad Steiner's kindly concern for the Palmer girl, I might have not learned about her dead husband until it was too late.

I tried again to call Jed Furst, the insurance man from Amalgamated National, and this time he answered on the fourth ring. After I explained who I was, and that I was working for Ag-Mach, he seemed willing enough to help if he could. I told him that I wasn't getting much cooperation from the warehousemen at Shed Fourteen, and they had a grouch about losing their overtime payments.

"According to them," I enlarged, "they always did the night loading until a few months ago. Then they were suddenly told that the company insurance didn't cover evening work, and it would have to be done by the company's customers. I don't know how true that is, but that's what they say."

He didn't answer right away, but then he said.

"Look, Mr Preston, I don't want to seem uncooperative, but you have to remember I deal with thousands of policies. I can't carry that kind of detail around in my head. Why don't you call me at the office tomorrow? All my files are there, and I'll be able to answer a question like that right off the bat."

It was a perfectly reasonable reaction, but I didn't want to lose the time unless it was forced on me.

"I appreciate that, I really do," I assured him, "but these circumstances were kind of unusual. I thought it might have stuck in your mind. The

way its told to me, your company has
always carried the cover for Ag-Mach,
and there hadn't been any query for
years. Then, all of a sudden, and
only a few months back, Amalgamated
decided that this late-night work wasn't
covered by the policy. I know you have
a lot of cases to think about, but wasn't
this a little bit out of the usual run?"

Again there was silence, and I
thought he was getting me ready for
the bounce. Then he came back.

"Wait a minute, there was something,
now that you remind me. And you're
right about it being unusual. Yes, yes
I do have some recall on this, and
I'll tell you why. You see, in this
business what usually happens is that
somebody makes a claim, and when
they find out the policy doesn't cover
the circumstances, they get upset. It
happens all the time, just because
people haven't bothered to read the
conditions properly."

I was glad he couldn't see my face.
As an automobile owner I've suffered

that one myself with painful results.

"Yes," I encouraged, "I understand that."

"Right, well that's why I now remember this business with the Ag-Mach people. They made the call first. That is to say, they suddenly came to me and said, look, we're doing this work at nights, and we're not sure it's covered by the policy. Would I confirm? Well, you can bet I would, and sure enough they weren't covered by the terms. I told them it was easy to correct. All they had to do was to advise me in writing, and in advance, when they intended to do this kind of work, and then they would be covered. I wrote them a letter, to explain all this, and I never heard any more about it."

"Did they say why they raised it with you in the first place?" I pressed.

"Not that I recall. Mark you, it was a sensible thing to do. If more of our clients made these simple enquiries, we'd have a lot less disputes to deal with."

Hooray for Ag-Mach, I reflected.

"And, of course, after all these months, you wouldn't bring to mind the person who approached you?"

"No," he said doubtfully, "no, I don't think — wait a minute, yes I do, though. You're absolutely right, and it is unusual. The enquiry didn't originate with the client. It's all coming back to me now. What happened was, there was another company, somebody Ag-Mach was doing business with. They wanted to know what the insurance position was on this evening work. It was for their own protection you see. Yes," he confirmed, "I can recall the whole thing now. It started with these other people, definitely. They explained all the details to me, and I had no option but to say that the policy would not cover such a variety of circumstances."

"This other company," I pressed gently. "You wouldn't happen to recall the name?"

"Not offhand," he regretted. "There'll be a note on the file, though, if you care to call me tomorrow. Some export people, as I recall, but as I say, I'd need the file. It was a woman I spoke with. Nice voice."

I didn't need his file. It would have come as a terrible surprise to me if the export people he referred to were any other than the Monkton Export Company. I thanked Mr Furst at some length, and I meant it. He said it was a pleasure, and made a half-hearted attempt to sell me some life-cover, with a bonus element that would rock the financial structure of the western world. If I lived to be a hundred and ten, that was.

After we hung up, I began to feel that we might be getting somewhere. For my guess, Monkton Export had presented a case to Mr Furst in such a way that he could not possibly have let Amalgamated National be responsible for insurance cover. They would have asked him to make this clear in writing to Ag-Mach, and that meant Dexter Hadley, or Deputy Financial

Administrator. That left the way clear for the two ware housemen, Jenks and Genette, to be told they couldn't be used on the overtime work any longer. It also left the way clear for other people to have the run of Shed Fourteen, and to do whatever it was they wanted to do, with no one else around to see them doing it.

Like drilling holes.

It had to be the holes. There's nothing very secret or confidential about shifting a damned great hunk of machinery like an earth-mover. It really couldn't be important whether the AG4B was driven out and loaded onto the ship by Ag-Mach people or the export people. What was important was that they needed some time, some unobserved time, alone with that machine. The overtime ban was just the ploy they required. As to the lady with the pleasant voice, I'd already begun to form half an opinion about her.

Pete Kowalski had said there was a woman working with his employers.

She would have to be an unusual woman to be in on something as complicated as this was beginning to sound. She'd need to know a little about business matters to come up with the idea of the insurance policy. When you took those factors, and added them to the unpleasant revelation that Kowalski had known who I was, you had to think of a woman who could fit into all three categories. There was only one female in this whole caper so far who met all the requirements. Especially the one about putting the finger on me.

Her name was Margaret Fordyce.

She not only knew about my existence, she also had a close idea of what I was doing. It would be a simple matter for her to keep tabs on my movements. She wouldn't even need to put someone on my tail all the time. There were only certain places I could go, certain people I could talk to. My whole pattern was more or less prescribed by the facts of the enquiry. Damn it, I'd even done some of their work for them by locating Suzanne Palmer. All they had to do in that case was to tag along behind, and quietly waste the girl at their leisure. It had nearly come off too, if I hadn't got lucky.

I was beginning to get angry, sitting there. Nobody likes to be the patsy, and I'm no different from the next man. It was especially galling to have to view Margaret Fordyce from this new angle. Any mental plans I may have entertained for that lady had been vastly different from the vengeful images which were now passing through my head. Anger is an unprofitable area for me. Sometimes it is possible to give vent to it, with varying results. Mostly, it has to be contained, like now. Contained, you understand, not dismissed. Contain and channel, that's the process. After a few minutes of useless fuming, I put the cork on, and brought my mind back to practicalities.

It had been a lucky shot for me when I accused Kowalski of having murdered Larry Palmer. Up until that time I had no evidence that the man was a murder victim. It was just one of those reasonable hunches, and it had paid off. The point was, why? Palmer hadn't been anybody special. A harmless draughtsman, who spent his spare time dreaming up war machines, was a little out of the usual run of people to be eliminated. There was no question of a sudden outburst of temper, a quick gunshot, or any of those things which are at the root of so much sudden death. Palmer's murder must have been planned with great care, and sufficient expertise to have fooled the police into accepting an accidental death verdict. Therefore, someone not only wanted him out of the way, but also wanted no undue attention given to the man. Once the people from Homicide start digging around, there's no telling what they might turn up, so the thing to do was to avoid their involvement. At least it told me one thing, with fair certainty. There was something to be learned from Larry Palmer, dead or not, and I had better set about finding out what it was.

I didn't think there was much more that Suzanne could have told me. To her, Larry was a man who played with submarines, in much the same way that some people collect stamps or old coins. Her interest hovered around the zero level. Who then, could I tackle? The most obvious and fruitful choice would have been Dexter Hadley, but he'd already gone the same route as Palmer. There was still Walter Sturges, and I'd already tried once to call him, earlier in the evening.

Time for another try. Anything would be an improvement on planning various oriental tortures for Margaret Fordyce. This time I got him on the third brr and he wasn't pleased.

"Preston? Listen, I'm right in the middle of the double-header," he protested. "Couldn't this wait till morning?"

"Things are moving faster than I expected, Walt," I said smoothly. "Sorry to interrupt the game, but I need some information."

"Well," he sighed, "if you need it, I guess you need it What's the problem?"

"This is strictly between us, O.K.?"

"If you say so. What's the mystery?"

I told him I kept coming across the name of Larry Palmer, and wanted to know more about him.

"Palmer?" he echoed. "Mystery is right. Where does he fit in to this?"

"I don't know that he does," I denied, "but I'd like to eliminate him, if I can. Did he work for you?"

"In a way. Larry was in the Design Department, and I keep a sort of eye on that."

"But not Hadley?" I pressed. "He didn't come under Hadley?"

"Certainly not," he denied. "Hadley was Finance."

"Then how come Hadley dealt with the widow, and not you?"

I could picture his face, as he tried to work out where all this was leading.

"Simple," he replied. "I was out of the country. On business. Dexter Hadley did me a favour by looking after the widow and everything."

"I see. Did you know Palmer was always experimenting with military designs? Aircraft, submarines and so forth?"

"Certainly," he confirmed. "Everybody knew that. He had this thing about people stealing his ideas. I told him if ever he wanted to register a patent he should talk to Hadley. Dex would look after him, make sure he did it all according to the book."

"And did he?" I queried.

"Did who what?" he countered.

"Did Palmer ever come up with anything, and ask for Hadley's assistance? It could be important, Walt."

"Well now, I couldn't give you a definite yes or no to that." He sounded almost regretful. "You see, Larry Palmer was a nice guy, and

I mean that, but on this question of patents he was almost paranoid. What I'm saying is, even if he did come up with something, he wouldn't have confided in me. I guess we'll never know the answer to that one. The only person who could have been liable to help you was Dex Hadley. You still haven't said what makes it important. Are you thinking that Larry Palmer could in some way have been responsible for those crazy holes?"

"Tell you the truth, I don't know what I think," I admitted. "I seem to be going around in circles. Well, I'd better let you get back to your game. Thanks for the help. We'll just forget we talked, O.K.?"

"If you say so," he agreed. "I don't see what's such a big deal."

"Let me put it this way," I suggested. "I wouldn't want it to get around that I'm spending so much time running up blind alleys. It could be bad for my reputation."

He gave a short laugh.

"It'll cost you a beer sometime."

"You got it."

I sat there, reflecting that there was more truth than I cared to admit in that crack about blind alleys. If Palmer had been on the invention route, and if he'd confided in Dexter Hadley, I was going to have the devil of a job finding out. Both the principal actors were dead, murdered, and that's as blind an alley as you can get.

The only new name I had was that of Tom Brewer, of the Monkton Export Co. I would have liked a chat with Tom, but the way things were shaping, we'd be liable to be doing our talking from the wrong ends of pistols. He would know about Kowalski in the near future, and it wouldn't take him long to work out how his man came to wind-up in the hospital. It came to me, rather late in the day, that I might have become a prime target myself. These people had already killed twice, and would have made it three times, if I hadn't been there to save

Suzanne Palmer. If they'd been willing to do that to her, when she seemed to know nothing at all, they wouldn't think twice about hitting me. Asking questions and making trouble is my business, and they couldn't afford to run the risk that I might stumble across something. On the whole, it might be prudent for me to spend the night away from the apartment.

I took a spare box of ammo from the drawer, in case I got involved in some kind of shooting war. For a few moments, I toyed with the idea giving Brewer to the police. If he was involved in Palmer's death, as Kowalski had claimed, then strictly speaking it was a job for Homicide. On the other hand, with Palmer's death so long behind, and people's memories being what they are, there probably wouldn't be enough for the D.A. to make out a reasonable case. Brewer would be back on the street within hours, and fully alerted. He, and whoever was involved with him, would tread very softly for a while, and that wouldn't suit my book at all.

No, things were best left. I needed Brewer and his associates to be going about their business without the extra caution that police attention would bring. When people are doing nothing at all, they can't make mistakes. What I wanted was mistakes, and the more the merrier.

As I was about to leave the apartment, the phone rang. It was Sam Thompson.

"Glad I caught you," he greeted, "you going to be home for a while? Wanna make a report."

"You're supposed to be keeping an eye on Mrs Hadley," I said testily.

"That's what I want to report about," he returned, unperturbed. "Shall I come round there?"

"No," I decided. "I'm just going out. Tell you what, I'll be at the Gipsy Caravan at eleven. Meet me there. Oh, and Sam — "

"Yeah?"

"Are you carrying anything?"

"No," he replied. "I didn't think it would be necessary, just to keep an eye on some poor widow lady."

"Things have warmed up a little," I advised him. "I wouldn't want you to be uncomfortable."

"I'll be comfortable," he promised. "Eleven it is."

10

I TOOK a room at the Hotel Paradiso before keeping my appointment with Thompson. Then I drove the eight miles out of town, to where the Gipsy Caravan is situated. It lies back from the highway, and holds a good position below the hills, so that it is sheltered from any sudden storms blowing in from the ocean. As caravans go, it is one of the more advanced variety, consisting of two stories of concrete, steel and glass, and without a wheel in sight. The gipsies all have names like Boris and Andrei, but the native tongue is pure West Coast. They have a little band up in one corner, all balalaikas and accordions, and the tables are covered with bright red check cloths. It all seemed a long way from the Hungarian forests.

Sam Thompson was draped across

the bar, a half-empty stein of beer within reach. I parked on the next stool, and picked up a handful of pretzels.

"Be careful you don't work too hard," I greeted him.

He turned his head and inspected me impassively.

"This was your idea," he pointed out. "Personally, I don't like the place. I always expect the Wolf Man to come in and snatch one of the girls."

"Only on gala night," I replied, "and this isn't Saturday. So how come you're not doing what I asked?"

He looked offended then, as if I was attacking his professional behaviour.

"It's done," he said shortly, "I went out to Oak Valley, to the address you gave me. There was nobody home, but I got lucky. There's a woman lives in the next apartment, a regular little curtain-twitcher. She came out and asked me what I wanted with poor Mrs Hadley. I told her I was from poor Mr Hadley's office, and we needed to be in touch with the widow. She said she had this telephone number where I could reach the lady if it was really urgent. Mrs Hadley had gone to stay with some old friends for a few days, what with the shock and all, but she supposed it would be O.K. to give me the number, my being from the company and everything."

I nodded.

"Sounds reasonable. Could I have the number?"

Now he looked aggrieved.

"There's more," he told me. "I didn't think you'd settle for a telephone number. You might have wanted some of your money back, and that could have been difficult. I checked the number out, and it belongs to a party named Arnold Hall, with an address on Palm Drive. I went over and took a look at the place. Very exclusive, very expensive."

"I know the neighborhood," I chimed in. "Maybe Mrs Hadley and Mrs Hall were at school together, something like that."

He shook his head, evidently impatient that I should interrupt the flow.

"That's just it," he corrected. "There isn't any Mrs Hall. There isn't anybody at the house except Arnold Hall himself."

"Well, maybe the old man was a friend of Dexter's."

"The old man," he advised me, speaking slowly, "is thirty-eight years old, and lives like a movie star. I ran a check on him. He has a rating of Gold Plus Double A, and is good news at any place in town."

It seemed to suggest that the grieving widow was making a fast recovery. It also reminded me that Dexter Hadley had been worried about his wife's activities. What Sam Thompson was now telling me was what Hadley had hired me to find out.

"So the poor guy was right," I muttered.

"Huh? What poor guy?" Thompson looked worried.

"Nothing. Just thinking out loud.

You've done well, Sam. looks as if I don't need to worry too much about the lady being overcome with grief."

He nodded solemnly.

"Know what I wondered? It's just this nasty old mind I have. I wondered whether this Hall might know a little something about what happened to the late Hadley. I mean, if he's playing Call the Doctor with Mrs Hadley, he might have decided that Mr Hadley was a nuisance. It's happened before."

I shook my head in rebuttal.

"This isn't that kind of thing. There were two guns used to kill Hadley. He wasn't bumped off by any jealous lover. Besides, the body was driven out to that waste ground and dumped. That's gang stuff, a business killing."

He sighed, unconvinced.

"If you say so. All I know is, guys will do the craziest things when there's a dame in the background. Still, it's your case, not mine. I guess I'm through now, huh?"

He said it without much conviction.

There had to be more, or I wouldn't have asked him to carry a gun.

"Not quite. Since Mrs Hadley is busy elsewhere, that means the apartment is empty. I'd like to take a little nose around over there. Dexter Hadley got hold of some papers, and it could be useful if I got a look at them."

The sleepy eyes widened slightly.

"I don't know," he hedged. "Sounds like a one man job to me. You don't really need two of us just to go looking for some papers. Besides, it's kind of illegal. I have to think of my good name."

"It's worth another fifty," I told him. "And you don't have to do anything illegal. I just want to be able to feel that my back is safe. There are certain other people very interested in all these goings on, and they kill. I don't want them killing me. All you have to do is keep watch."

"Seventy-five," he countered.

"You're a thief Sam."

"Harsh words. Besides, I would have

thought your back was worth a measly seventy-five dollars. Think of it as insurance."

It was just after eleven-thirty when we reached Oak Valley, and Thompson guided me to the apartment building. Several of the windows were in darkness, and we sat there studying the layout. It was a narrow block, with just four apartments to each floor. The elevators and stairway were centrally placed, so that at each level there were two apartments, one each side. Thompson pointed upwards.

"The one next to the elevators is where the nosey neighbor lives. The Hadleys are next door, and that gives them the side windows."

There was a fire stairway running down the side of the building, but I wasn't enthusiastic about going up that way. There was a certain amount of light from the street, and the odds on being spotted by some casual observer were too great. If the exterior darkness of the windows was anything to judge by, the lady in the next apartment would appear to have retired for the night. My best bet was to go in through the front door, and trust that she was not a light sleeper. I couldn't risk the elevator, I decided. If her apartment was next to it, the noise could easily disturb her.

"I'm going up the stairs," I said. "Don't fall asleep on me Sam. The opposition could be around, and they play rough."

There was no one around to take any interest in my arrival. I went up the stairs carefully, leaving two elevators open and waiting in the foyer. When I reached my floor, I paused in the corridor, listened intently, with my hand pressed against the side wall of the apartment belonging to the inquisitive neighbour. The fact that there were no lights showing was not conclusive, in my experience. Some people prefer to watch T.V. in the darkness, especially older people, because it's the closest they can get to the old movie-going habit. No sound was coming through the wall. I walked very slowly along to apartment 8a, pausing at each step and listening. Sam Thompson had told me what kind of door-lock to expect, and I had a small collection of master-keys with me. The second one fitted, and I turned the catch soundlessly, letting myself into the darkened apartment. Not wanting to risk a light in the tiny hallway, I felt my way into a room and located a switch. It turned out to be the bathroom, but with the reflected light from the open doorway I was able to find my way to the living area, than the bedrooms. There were two, and things between Hadley and Joyce/Rosanna must have deteriorated further than he'd led me to believe. Both bedrooms had recently been in use, and might as well have been marked His and Hers. His was austere, not to say monk-like, and I went quickly through cupboards and drawers, finding little of interest, except that he was a conservative dresser at all times. I'd almost given up hope when I located the basket. It was a small wickerwork affair, balanced on the top shelf on his clothes closet. I lifted it down, and it was heavy for its size. There was a small lock on it, but Hadley had evidently not considered it necessary to make the basket secure. Placing it carefully on the bed, I lifted the lid.

Most prowlers would not consider a pile of books very exiting, but I was no ordinary prowler. I was looking at Larry Palmer's collection of military hardware manuals, and it pleased me. I didn't know why it should please me, except that Palmer had thought the books important, and Hadley had been of the same opinion. He'd thought they were important enough to remove from the Palmer household as soon as the owner was dead. With any luck at all, I was about to find out why.

Sitting on the bed, I picked up the first one. It was entitled 'Warplanes of the Past', and I began to turn the pages, with no clear idea of what I hoped to find. Then I paused, thinking. If I was going to study each page in each volume, I'd be sitting there most of the night. Maybe there was a short cut. Maybe if I shook each book, some paper marker might fall out. I wasn't too hopeful of a successful result, but it was better than page-turning. I riffled quickly through 'Warplanes', then held the volume upside down, shaking. Nothing happened. I drew a blank with the next, and two more after that, and was starting to visualise a night of study after all, when I got something. It was the fifth volume, and as I bent the pages back to flick them through, the book fell naturally open in my hands. There was a photograph at the head of each page, and two columns of figures and description below. Between the two pages lay a folded sheet of graph paper. There seemed to be some kind of drawing on the inserted sheet, but I put that to one side for the moment, and concentrated on the photographs.

Each was of a heavy-looking tank, and to my inexperienced eye they looked identical. However, according to the captions, they were respectively the Smetana Mark IX and the Smetana Mark VII. Smetana?

In my haste, I hadn't bothered to look at the title of the book. I turned back to the front cover. The title was 'Eastern Bloc Hardware', and the photographs were of what was described as 'Bulgarian' tanks. Now I unfolded the graph paper and a sectional diagram lay before me. It looked for all the world like a taper-fronted wheelbarrow, except that there was no wheel, and it made no sense at all. Still, I had something, whatever it was, and this was no time for speculation. I put book and drawing to one side, and carried on with the search. Nothing else came to light, and I had to make a decision. Either I would take a chance that what I had found would prove to mean something, or I could stay put and carry out the page by page inspection.

I decided to take a chance.

Quickly, I restored the rest of the books to the basket, and put it back in place. Finished now, with Hadley's bedroom, I had a quick look at the rest of the apartment. There wasn't much to be learned, except that they seemed to read a lot, and enjoyed early American furniture. The wife's bedroom was frilly but not excessively so. She had a lot of clothes, mostly with good name-tags, but there was very little jewellery on display. Her perfumes were French, and the air in the room was heady. I found myself wondering about her, which was unprofitable. I knew all I needed to know about Joyce, call-me-Rosanna, Hadley, and I didn't like her. Whatever else Dexter Hadley may have been up to, he had deserved a little more support on the domestic front than he seemed to have been getting. In the living room, I found a studio photographic portrait of the happy pair, and finally got a look at her face. She was a striking looking woman, no question about it. Although she was smiling in the picture, the face was dominated by her eyes. They were large, and somehow conveyed a sense of troubled depths. Whatever the rest of her features might be doing, you knew somehow that the key to what was going on in her mind lay in those strange orbs. It was almost as though she could see me, an intruder in her apartment, and I looked quickly away, with the strangest feeling of unease. It was time to get out. Over the years I've often found myself in the position of searching through somebody else's home, but it's never become routine. There is always this lurking sense of disquiet, this knowledge of personal wrong, no matter what the justification.

Scooping up my book, and marking the place with the drawing, I switched off the lights and left. Despite my great care, the front door of their apartment made the tiniest of clicks as I shut it, and I went quickly away, before the lady next door had time to investigate.

"What the hell kept you?" demanded Thompson nervously. "I was beginning to think somebody must have been waiting for you up there."

I got into the car, staring up at the face of the block. No lights had been switched on in the next door apartment, so evidently I had not disturbed the neighbor.

"Took longer than I thought," I told him.

"I know how it is when you're busy reading," he returned acidly. "What did you steal, a first edition?"

I tucked the book away. There was no point in Thompson knowing more than was absolutely necessary.

"It's a cook book," I replied. "I'm going to make some jam."

I pulled away from the kerb and headed into the middle of town.

"Where are we going?" asked my passenger.

"Home," I announced. "There's

nothing more we can do tonight."

"Are you sure?" he queried. "There's all kinds of places we didn't burgle yet."

"Maybe we'll do some more tomorrow. Get some sleep, Sam. Call the office in the morning, and I'll have something for you."

With Thompson gone, I began automatically to drive back to Parkside. Funny, the way the subconscious will take over, if your mind is busy on other things. I was actually turning into my home street when I remembered I wasn't planning on being there tonight. Ten minutes later, I was unlocking the door of my room of the Hotel Paradiso.

Safely inside, I opened up my precious book, and started to worry at it again. A man didn't have to be a great big detective to deduce that the drawing had been the work of Larry Palmer. The more I stared at it, the more it looked like the superstructure of a wheelbarrow. Maybe it was a wheelbarrow. Maybe it was just a drawing that Palmer had lying around, and he needed something to mark his place in the book.

Maybe.

And, then again, maybe what I needed was a second opinion. An opinion from somebody with a properly-trained mind. Like an engineer. Like Walter Sturges.

I still had his number in my pocket. It was a quarter to one in the morning, and he wasn't going to be best pleased to hear from me, but this was important. The telephone rang four times before there was a click. A machine said.

"This is Walter Sturges. I'm in bed asleep, and I have to work tomorrow. If your message is really urgent, please come and bang on my door. If not, why don't we just leave it till the morning? Have a nice night."

Despite myself, I grinned at the receiver. Sturges must be something of an amateur psychologist, I decided. People don't mind picking up a telephone, at any time of the day or night. But, faced with the necessity to go and call on a man, they might feel that perhaps their business could wait after all. It certainly applied in my case. I would have found it hard to justify hauling a man out of bed, just to look at a couple of pictures of Russian — sorry, Bulgarian — tanks. It would have to wait.

"Have a nice night yourself," I told the machine.

11

THE bedside telephone shrilled, and kept on shrilling.

"Well?" I growled.

"Seven-thirty, sir. Your call."

Seven-thirty? Had I really been so crazy as to leave a call for such an ungodly hour? Yes, I had, I admitted, and this was crunch-time. Swinging my legs out of bed I sat upright and waited for tomorrow to become today. There was something different about the apartment, for example, and in almost no time I recalled that I wasn't in the apartment at all, but in an hotel room. It's little things like that which take bringing into focus in those crucial early minutes.

Soon, I was sufficiently in touch to call Walter Sturges number. The cheerful voice, which had informed me he was asleep, had been replaced by a

240

less welcoming tone.

"Well?" he growled.

He didn't seem to bounce with joy when he learned who was calling, and was even less enthusiastic when he heard what I wanted.

"At this hour?" he demanded incredulously. "Some of us have jobs, you know. I'm due out at the plant."

"It's important, Walt," I assured him. "I wouldn't waste your time. And, don't forget, this is company business. It's Morton Weill I'm working for."

"Then why," he countered, "can't we just deal with whatever it is out at the plant?"

It was a reasonable question, and I paused before replying.

"All right, I'll tell you. The reason I don't want to do that is because I'm not sure who I can trust."

It was his turn to think. Then he said guardedly.

"What is that supposed to mean?"

I wasn't ready to voice my suspicions

about Margaret Fordyce. For one thing, I wasn't yet ready to back it up, and for another, I didn't want to risk putting that lady on the alert.

"I can't talk about it on the telephone," I hedged. "You can understand that I can't afford to take any chances. Two people have been murdered already, and I don't want to be the third."

"Two? Did you say two? Who's the other one?"

"I'll tell you when I see you," I promised. "Fifteen minutes?"

"I suppose so," he sighed. "Do you know where I live?"

I didn't, and he told me, and it was almost twenty minutes later when I reached the neat little farm house. The door opened at once, and Walt Sturges stood there, fully dressed, and waving me in. There was a strong smell of coffee in the house, and my stomach rolled about unhappily.

"Something smells good," I said hopefully.

He took me through into a bright cheerful room and waved me to a chair. Then he went away, and came back with two steaming cups. He made his coffee strong hot and bitter, which suited me fine.

"You said there's been another murder," he reminded. "Is it anybody I would know?"

I had to trust somebody, and this looked like the time. I told him about Larry Palmer, and his face registered disbelief.

"I wondered why you were asking all those questions about him last night, but I didn't expect anything like this. Are you sure?"

I nodded.

"Oh yes, I'm sure. I even know who killed him, and why."

His expression altered now to suspicion.

"If you know all that, why aren't you telling the police?"

"I'm not ready yet. I wasn't hired to find out who killed who. My job is to get an explanation for all the mystery out at the warehouse with the AG4B. Plus," I ploughed on, sensing another protest in the making, "I was doing something the police wouldn't like, when I found out about Palmer. Something they could lock me up for, if they were in a bad mood. I don't want to go near those people until I have the whole story."

He didn't like it, and he shook his head uncertainly.

"I don't like to get involved in this kind of thing," he stated. "Murder, policemen, all that stuff, that's not my scene. I'm just a simple engineer, and I'd like to keep it that way."

That cued me in to the purpose of the visit, and I hastened to reassure him.

"You're not involved, and you won't be. Only reason I told you was so that you'd appreciate the urgency. What I'm here about is engineering. The rest of this conversation never happened."

He seemed partly convinced.

"If you say so. What's the problem?"

I picked up my book and opened it at the picture of the Smetana tanks, keeping the drawing folded in my hand for the moment. He stared at the photographs.

"Tanks?" he said, in a surprised tone. "What about them?"

"I don't know," I admitted. "But they seemed to have been important to Palmer. He made this drawing."

I showed him my wheel-less wheelbarrow and he peered at it intently. His eyes went to the tanks, then back to the drawing.

"All right," he decided. "So I don't get it. What's supposed to be the connection?"

I was a little disappointed. I'd been half-hoping he might leap into the air, and come out with a detailed explanation. Instead, he was clearly as baffled as I had been.

"Damned if I know," I said grudgingly. "But there has to be one. Two men have died."

He inclined his head soberly, and

pored once more over the drawing.

"Let's try to visualise what this thing will look like when it's produced. One thing you always had to give Larry Palmer. He never omitted any detail. Hallo, that's odd."

I watched anxiously as he held the drawing away from his face and referred to the open book.

"Odd?" I prompted.

He sat down beside me, the book between us, and the drawing in his hands.

"That side measurement," he pointed. "Seven point four metres. It's the same as the overall length of the tank. And this width here — why it's almost as though — "

His voice tailed away as he worried at the solution, and he wasn't really talking to me in any case. He was now an engineer, with an engineer's problem, and his mind was too occupied to bother with externals. There are times for keeping quiet, and this was one of them.

Suddenly, he got to his feet, and walked to the window, staring out. I sat very still. His eyes were screwed up, as though he was exerting some mental pressure to squeeze an idea from the back of his mind.

"It's nonsense of course," he said absently, then turned and walked out of the room. I stayed where I was, very conscious that I had no contribution to make to the present situation. He seemed to be gone for a long time, and I waited there, finishing my coffee and smoking an Old Favorite. When he finally came back, he was carrying a glossy brochure, which he opened with a flourish.

"I knew that measurement was familiar."

I nodded encouragement, whilst trying to read the printing on the front cover of the brochure. It was the illustrated product-range of the Ag-Mach Company. Sturges opened it, and put it down where I could see front and side-view photographs, plus technical drawings, of the AG4B.

"Seven point four metres," he pointed.

I started at the earth-mover, hoping for a revelation, but I just don't have an engineering mind.

"You lost me, Walter," I admitted. "All I'm getting is that the AG4B is the same length as this Smetana tank. Where does that take us?"

He took a pencil from his inner pocket, and looked around for anything with a straight edge. Finding nothing, he went across to a bureau, and rummaged inside, returning with a small rule.

"I'm probably whistling into the wind," he observed, "but just try to picture this."

With swift precise strokes, he began to draw onto the picture of the AG4B. At first they were just lines, and it still made no sense, but Sturges wasn't drawing lines to no purpose. When he was satisfied, he put down the rule, and looked at me.

"What do you think?" he asked.

I started, and tried to make sense of what he'd done. All I could see were a lot of pencilled lines, which certainly spoiled some perfectly good photographs of the earth-mover. It was a shame to have to reject his eager anticipation.

"I'm sorry, I just don't get it."

With a little snort of exasperation, he took the brochure away from me, and began to shade in between the lines. The familiar appearance of the AG4B began to disappear behind the pencilled areas and something different seemed to emerge. In fact — I looked away, then back again. There was no doubt about it. I was looking at what could easily have been an intelligent child's impression of a Smetana tank. It was crude. There were large and important areas of difference, but, for all that, there was no avoiding the comparison.

"I see it," I admitted slowly, "but I still don't get it."

Walt Sturges clapped me excitedly on the shoulder.

"Try this."

Holding the pencil vertically he made little stabbing motions at the corners of what I had taken to be a wheelbarrow. Small black dots appeared after each pencil-jab.

"The holes, man," he said exultantly, "we found the holes."

"The holes," I repeated dutifully.

"Lordy, Preston, it was no loss to engineering when you decided to take a career in investigation. These plates, here in the drawing, they are designed to be fitted to the body of the AG4B. Those holes, the ones we've all been worrying about, they were put there so that the plates could be bolted on. The matching holes in the plates are right here on the drawing. See, here and here." More jabbing with the pencil. "A do-it-yourself tank kit. A child could put it together."

Now that we had the engineering explained, we could get down to the more obvious problems.

"Look, Walt, I'll take your word for

the mechanical side of this," I began placatingly, "but even so, where does it get us? You don't make a tank by sticking a few lumps of metal on to a piece of agricultural machinery."

"No, that's true." He furrowed his brow, and yanked his tie loose from the collar of his shirt. Sturges was getting into the spirit of the thing. "We have to think this through. I'll get more coffee."

Not to be outdone, I took off my jacket and lit another cigaret.

"Now then," he said, putting down cups, and beginning to sound like a lecturer. "We have this problem. Somebody, somewhere, wants to bolt a few steel plates on to the Ag-Mach AG4B. Who are they, and why do they want to do it?"

"We have a head start there," I reminded him, "because we know, or rather you know, where these machines are going. Let's start off with a rundown."

"Right," he agreed. "The sale of

this model is about evenly distributed between domestic and foreign. I suggest we forget about the domestic buyers for the present, and concentrate on overseas. Most of our exports go to the Central and South American markets. Does that suggest anything?"

"It reminds me that there is usually some kind of war or domestic revolution taking place in three or four different countries at any one time. I ought to tell you something at this point, Walt. I know that there are gun-runners in this picture somewhere. They've been pushing the usual stuff, handguns, rifles and so forth."

He looked at me quizzically.

"You don't exactly give much away, do you?"

"I hadn't thought it might be relevant, until the last five minutes." It sounded lame, and it was.

"H'm." He didn't sound very convinced. "Well, at least you've mentioned it now. And it leads into my next point. As you said, there's always unrest somewhere on the south continent, and mostly the equipment used is pretty basic. They seem to get hold of the simple hardware without much difficulty, the kind of portable arms you just referred to. But the heavy stuff is harder to come by. Big guns, armoured cars, tanks. Most of the equipment is out of date, even when they do have it. Consider the background. If you were involved in a shooting war, somewhere in rough country, and both sides were relying on small-arms for their weaponry, what an enormous advantage it would be to have an armoured mobile of some kind. Not a real tank, but a machine which could trample through the opposition without much damage. If you try to visualise the AG4B, with armour plating round it, and maybe a machine-gun fore and aft, coming at you in the forest, when all you have is a rifle, it's going to look rather formidable."

I conjured up a mental image, and Sturges was right. It was a Valley of the Blind situation, where the one-eyed man is king. An armoured earth mover might be a comical concept to a sophisticated military tactician. It wouldn't look so funny to a bunch of ragged revolutionaries in half-jungle country.

"You'd need a turret," I murmured, half to myself.

"The driving position is already glassed-in. A simple matter to substitute bullet-proof glass. Position a swivel-gun behind the driver. I tell you Mark, it can be done. Dammit, I believe it is being done. It has to be. It's the only explanation."

Listening to his contagious enthusiasm, and looking at the photographs and drawings, I knew he was right.

"Let's talk it through, then," I suggested cautiously. "First, we order an AG4B from Ag-Mach. We need arming plates, so we order these from some steelworks. The supplier doesn't have to know what they're for. When the machine is ready for shipping we have only one problem. We have to be certain those plates are ready to be fitted on by amateurs in a couple of hours. That means we have to do the drilling here, because it's a precision job, and it can't be left to chance."

He wagged his head up and down in agreement.

"And somebody made a mistake with the machine that went up to Canada. Something went adrift with the shipping instruction, and the wrong people got the delivery. That's when the whole thing first attracted attention. Oh, Lord."

He looked at me as though he'd eaten something nasty.

"What is it?"

"It's just dawned on me that Dexter Hadley must have been involved in all this. That's why you were quizzing me about his relationship with Larry Palmer. That's why he was killed, isn't it?"

"It certainly looks that way," I admitted. "I can't come up with any other explanation. As to why he was killed, I haven't worked that one out. It's possible he realised the scheme would have to be abandoned. Or he could just have lost his nerve, I really don't know. But he ties in with too many of the known facts. I have to assume he was an important piece of the organisation."

"Dexter Hadley." Sturges didn't want to believe it, but was too experienced a man to go against the facts. "I'd never have believed it. This will be another terrible blow to his wife."

I thought about the sorrowing widow, making the best she could of it with Arnold Hall and all his money, but I contrived to keep a straight face, as I said.

"Yes, it's going to be hard on her."

Walt held his altered photograph of the AG4B at arm's length, and stared at it with quiet triumph.

"Poor Palmer," he muttered. "He really did have an inventive flair, didn't he? What happens now?"

The question was perfectly natural, and I'd been working out mentally how to enlist his assistance a while longer.

"I want to keep this strictly between us for the next few hours. A day at the most. We're not past the post yet."

He nodded seriously.

"Quite understand," he agreed. "It's one thing to know all this, quite a different bag of beans to prove it. I'm sure Mr Weill will agree."

I'd half-expected something of the kind.

"Walter, we can't bring him into this, not even him. You see, all the indications are that there's some unknown person involved in this. I don't know who it is, but until I do, I can't take any chances."

It was clear from his face that he was going to give me an argument.

"Even so," he objected, "you can't suspect Mr Weill. It's ridiculous. Damnit, he owns the company, he's a rich man. He doesn't have to get mixed up in a dirty operation like this. I really don't see how you can expect me to — "

" — look at it this way," I cut in. "You're right about your boss. I don't see any connection between him and this conspiracy. That isn't the point. You're a technical man. You must be aware of just how easy it is these days to bug a man's office, his telephone, even his car. Believe me, you would be doing Morton Weill no favour by telling him all this. It's far more likely that you'd be putting his life in danger, not to mention your own."

The thought of his own danger hadn't entered his mind until that point.

"Oh come now, that's a bit strong," he protested.

"Think about it. Two men are dead already. These people have an organisation to protect. They're not going to be too particular about getting rid of anyone who stands in the way."

I'd been lucky with Walter Sturges.

The various emotions which flitted across his face shifted between perplexity, anger and frustration. There was no fear.

"If I accept what you say," he pointed out, "then I'm in trouble already. You could have been followed here."

"No." I denied. "I spent last night at an hotel, and for two reasons. One was so these hoodlums wouldn't be able to find me. The other is that the police are probably looking for me by now, and I'm not ready for them yet. You're quite safe, Walt, so long as this remains between us. Do we have a deal?"

"I don't know," he hedged. "This is a big thing to keep to myself. Suppose something happens to you. What do I do then?"

I didn't care for the suggestion, but it was fair.

"You go straight to John Rourke, Captain of Detectives, Homicide Division, and tell him the whole tale. But meantime, there's something more practical for you to do."

I learned a long time ago that people like Sturges have an automatic favorable reaction to the word 'practical'.

"What is it?"

"Make an analysis of the sales of the AG4B for the past six months to the foreign market, with a separate note about the shipping companies involved, and freight loading times. That way, we ought to be able to estimate how many earth-movers are now doing duty as part-time tanks."

"And what will you be doing?"

I showed him my teeth.

"What I'm good at," I told him. "I may not be too bright about engineering drawings and that kind of stuff, but making trouble, that's different. These people have been calling the shots long enough, and disappearing back into the woodwork. I come from a long line of wood renovators. It's time I went to work."

He didn't seem too impressed with the idea.

"You think that's wise?" he queried.

"After all, they've already killed two people, that we know of. Wouldn't it be better just to let the police handle it from here?"

"Handle what?" I countered. "We don't have a damned thing we can prove. One move from the police, and this crowd will scuttle back into their holes. They're jumpy enough as it is. Somebody has to go out and provoke them, and I guess I'm elected. Don't look so worried Walt. This is what I get paid for."

I gathered up the books and the drawing, and tucked them under my arm. He walked with me to the street door.

"You'll let me know how it comes out?"

I promised him that I would, and left.

12

IT was too early yet for most offices to be at work, so I stopped in at a diner to get breakfast, picking up a copy of the Monkton City Globe on my way. Shad Steiner had done me proud, although the police department might take another view. They would have no doubt about where the story came from, but I knew I could rely on Steiner to hide behind the old tag of not revealing his sources.

When I finished eating, I put in a call to the office and spoke to Florence Digby. She told me the police had been asking about me, and I was to call them right away. I told her to forget we'd spoken, but that Sam Thompson would be getting in touch at any minute. Then I told her what I wanted him to do, and made her repeat it carefully. After that I killed time until ten o'clock, then presented myself at the offices of the Monkton Export Company. I asked for Mr Brewer, and gave my name as Harrigan.

"Tell him I have some news from the hospital," I told the girl at the desk.

She looked doubtful, but went away and reappeared two minutes later, holding the door for me.

"Mr Brewer doesn't usually see people without an appointment, Mr Harrigan, but when I mentioned the hospital he said he would give you three minutes. Straight through the main office, and it's the door facing you."

I thanked her, and went into a large room, where half a dozen people were too busy with their work to take any notice of me. At the end was a closed door, with the legend 'Manager' stencilled on it. For the benefit of the staff I gave a quick rap before opening it and stepping inside. There was another door at the far end of the room, but my eyes were absorbed with the man at the desk.

Tom Brewer was a smooth-cheeked man of forty, with thinning dark hair combed carefully over bald patches. He had quick darting eyes, which took in every square inch of me within seconds.

"Mr Harrigan? What's all this about the hospital?"

I made no answer, but sat down, resting my books on the desk, and lighting up an Old Favorite. He watched the performance with some impatience.

"Kowalski made a statement," I told him finally.

The news didn't seem to cause him much alarm.

"A statement, you say? What about?"

"About the whole thing," I smiled. "You're all washed up, Brewer. The lid is off."

"Look here Harrigan," he said, unperturbed, "you're not making any sense. I don't know what you're talking about, so kindly get out of my office. What's that?"

I opened up the Ag-Mach catalogue

and showed him the photograph which Walter Sturges had scribbled on. His face went tight.

"I don't understand," he blurted out, but without conviction.

"Sure you do, Tom," I corrected. "Like I told you, Kowalski made a full statement. About the gunrunning, about Palmer's murder, everything."

He swallowed quickly, but he wasn't going to give in that easily. A manicured hand waved at me.

"This is all gibberish to me. Mr Kowalski was one of our outside employees. I know nothing about his activities, as I've already explained to the police."

I laughed in admiration, shaking my head.

"You'll sound good in court, Tom, I'll say that for you. But it's gone too far. Pete Kowalski blew the whistle on you, because he thought he was going to die. Told me the whole thing. Told me how you and the woman killed Palmer. Why did you do that, Tom?

It would have been simpler just to give the poor guy a small cut. I wouldn't be here now if you'd done that. As it is — "

I shrugged, and left him to complete the sentence.

"I've never heard of this Palmer, whoever he is — "

" — was — "

" — was, then. Why don't you go to the police with these fairy tales? They deal with lunatics every day."

I gave him a little derisive snort.

"Police? Who needs those people? No, you have this all wrong, Tom. I don't want the police, anymore than you do. What I want is in. This is a nice set-up you have. Good, legitimate business out there. Nice profitable side-line, in here. I don't want to make waves. Kowalski said he was going to take off. Thought you'd probably kill him. That makes you a man short, and it's your lucky day. Here I am."

He puckered up his forehead in three great wrinkles.

"Harrigan, you say? You're talking nonsense, of course, but I'm intrigued to know where you fitted in with Kowalski. I've never heard of you."

"Neither had Kowalski, till last night," I explained, watching those quicksilver eyes. "We got to know each other after I shot him."

He stiffened then, and some of his composure drained away.

"You shot him?" he repeated, more to himself than me.

"Oh yes, didn't I mention that? He was trying to kill Palmer's widow at the time, and I didn't think he should. So, like I say, shot him. Then I took the girl away, to a safe place. She's my little bit of insurance, in case you get nasty with me. Don't worry about her, she doesn't want any trouble."

A thick pink tongue emerged slowly from the full lips and made a nervous circuit of his mouth.

"I wonder whether I heard the name right. Harrigan? Are you sure it isn't Preston? Mark Preston?"

"Mostly it's Preston," I agreed.

"I thought it must be," he nodded. "And I think we've heard enough. You should have walked while you could. Too late now."

Almost casually, he produced a large blue-steel revolver and pointed it at me over the desk. One shot would have blown away half my chest.

"What's that for?" I asked. "Those people out in the main office aren't all deaf."

The gun didn't scare me too much. The men and women I'd passed on my way to his office were ordinary working people, not gangsters. Brewer might be the manager, but they weren't going to keep quiet if he started blowing holes in the visitors. I was puzzled as to what he expected to gain by this flourish.

Then the door at the far end of the room opened and another man walked in, a stranger. He was six feet tall, immaculate in a cream tropic suit, and there was authority in the arrogantly handsome face.

"I'm sorry about this, but you heard what he said."

Brewer spoke to the newcomer without taking his eyes off me.

"Yes, indeed."

White suit showed me a small pearl-handled automatic as he walked around behind me. Cold metal pressed against the base of my neck.

"Quite still, if you please."

Tanned fingers appeared over my shoulder and disappeared inside my coat, locating the thirty-eight. I felt a sense of loss as the familiar weight was lifted out.

"There now," mocked the pleasant voice. "You'll be more comfortable without this. Oh, what a good drawing. Did you do that, Mr Preston?"

He was clear of me now, and staring at Walter Sturges' work.

"No," I denied. "You'd better start worrying about the man who did."

"Oh, I shall, I shall," he assured me. "But I have this rule. I only worry about one thing at a time. Right at this moment, my main worry is you. I think we ought to go somewhere and have a little chat."

While he was talking, he was busy slotting metal on to the little automatic. There was a smooth click and he smiled.

"There now. I'm sure a man of your experience knows a silencer when he sees one. I don't want to have to shoot you, not yet, but I will if you attempt anything foolish. We're going to leave now, and I want you to understand something. If you so much as cough, I will certainly use this thing. Get up."

I stayed where I was.

"I don't like to be shot by strangers," I objected. "Just who the hell are you?"

He looked faintly surprised.

"You mean you don't know? Well, that's good. That's very good. I always try to keep a low profile in these matters, and it would seem that it works. Oh, by the way, if you're not on your feet by the time I count to three,

I shall put a bullet in your hand."

There are threats and threats. Given a choice, I'll take the loud, blustering kind any time. The deadly casualness of White Suit told me to do what he said. I got up. So did Brewer, putting the revolver into his waistband.

"I'd better bring the pictures," he said, gathering up my stuff. "Don't want the staff coming in here poking around while I'm gone."

"Let Mr Preston carry them," instructed his boss. "They are his property after all, and it'll occupy one of his arms."

He motioned with the gun, and I scooped up the book and the catalogue.

"This way." White-Suit pointed to the rear door. "There's a very good service elevator at the rear, and we shan't need to bother the staff."

Brewer led the way, with me behind him, and White-Suit completing the procession. The elevator was small, but there was no opportunity for me to attempt anything. The man with the silencer was taking no chances.

At street level, Brewer stepped out, looking both ways.

"All clear," he announced. "Which car?"

"We'll take mine. It'll probably be Mr Preston's last ride, and we ought to make him as comfortable as we can."

Things were not going my way at all. White-Suit had a brand-new Cadillac in the rear park, and I could scarcely expect Sam Thompson to be in two places at once. He would be watching the front of the building by now, and he wasn't a clairvoyant. As I climbed into the rear of the car, some of my confidence was beginning to disappear. The boss man got in beside me, instructing Brewer to drive.

"Where are we going?" I queried, as we threaded our way out of the business district.

White-Suit was at the far end of the seat, and half-turned towards me, obviating any possibility of a quick lunge at him. Now he frowned.

"We shall go to my house," he

informed me. "It's quiet there, and no one will hear you yell."

The prospect held little attraction.

"Oh? Am I going to be yelling?"

"I'm afraid so," he confirmed. "You don't strike me as being very much of a realist, Preston. I want to know things, things that only you can tell me. A realist, in your situation, would tell me at the outset. He would know that he's going to tell me eventually, so why should he suffer a lot of pain? It's all so pointless. But you, I suspect will prefer the hard way."

I let him talk. My mind was busy on more urgent matters, such as, how did I expect to get out of this? In the office, I hadn't been too concerned about Brewer and his gun. I'd provoked him into doing what I hoped would be something foolish, so that his hand would be forced, and he'd lead me to the top man. Sam Thompson had been waiting outside for precisely that eventuality. I hadn't bargained on the office being rigged, with the top man close at hand, and listening to every word. Instead of being in control of a situation I'd planned, I now found myself in a very different ball-game, and no one to carry it but me. Thompson would still be back there, admiring the front of the building.

We were in residential country now, and the properties were spread well apart. The Caddy slowed, and turned right up a narrow blacktop, halting finally outside a pleasant-looking white-walled house. My escort made no move until Brewer climbed out, and opened the rear door. Then he handed the automatic to the waiting manager.

"Take this, in case our visitor gets brave while I'm climbing out. He won't get many more chances."

White-Suit was a thinker. I'd been weighing up my chances of diving at him in those crucial seconds as he got out of the car. By getting rid of the hardware, he'd taken any value out of the idea. Now, they were both standing there, waving me to follow.

Reluctantly, I got out, stretching my muscles in the sunshine. White-Suit went in through the front door, and I tagged along behind, with Brewer bringing up the rear.

There was a smell of perfume in the house, and it was somehow familiar. White-Suit pointed to a chair, and I sat down. We were at the back of the house now, on a sun-terrace. There was white-painted furniture scattered around, and a blue pool that shimmered invitingly. Close to the pool, a woman was stretched out on a yellow beach-lounger, taking the sun. What I could see of her body looked good, but the half-turned face was hidden under enormous dark glasses, and one of those floppy straw hats.

"Now," said my host, "let's get down to our little chat. How did you stumble across our little venture, Preston?"

"Piece here, and a piece there," I replied. "It would take too long to remember it all. There are too many people involved, and I like to have my little secrets. One thing you can be certain of, bumping me off is going to do you no good at all."

He laughed. It was a confident, pleasant sound, and it rang jarringly in my ears.

"The next thing you'll be telling me is that you've left secret instructions with your lawyer, who will take them to the police if you don't claim them before nightfall. Come along now, Preston, let us stick to realities."

"All right," I nodded, taking out my Old Favorites. "Let's do that. I'm a realistic kind of man. I'm the only one who knows what's going on outside. There are several people who know little pieces about all this, and I know who they are. Instead of waving artillery at me, you'd do better to wave your cheque book. Kill me, and those people are going to wonder. It'll only be a question of time before they do their wondering to the law. On the other hand, if you put a few dollars in my direction, I can be a useful man to have around."

Brewer sat at a table several feet away. He still had the automatic with the silencer, resting on a table inches away from his hand. Inside his coat was the big revolver he'd produced in the office. That meant White-Suit was unarmed, but I didn't see much profit in the situation. Brewer was safe from me, where he was sitting, and he was the man that mattered. His eyes never left me.

White-Suit looked thoughtful.

"A few dollars, you say? How few did you have in mind?"

I waved a hand around to indicate the surroundings.

"Think what's at risk," I suggested. "All this, plus a gun-running operation, not to mention a couple of murder-charges. I'm a reasonable man.

"Let's say a quarter-million."

His eyes went wide, and then he chuckled. So did the woman, with a low throaty sound.

"You call that reasonable?" queried the head man. "Well, I'm afraid I don't agree. You see, whatever it is you know, I shall know within an hour. And for nothing. I'm quite an expert on interrogation techniques, and I enjoy the work. I'm afraid you won't enjoy it quite so much. Tom."

Brewer got up then, the automatic level, and pointing at my head. White-Suit went into the house, and came back with a small suitcase. Resting the case on one of the little tables, he snapped it open, and tipped it so I could look inside. It looked like an emergency medical kit, all little tubes and needles. He took out a hypo and began to screw a long thin needle into place.

"I ought to be using gloves really," he explained casually. "But I don't think you and I need to concern ourselves about a few germs."

The needle went into a small bottle, and White Suit pulled carefully at the plunger. I watched, fascinated, as a pale milky fluid began to fill up the syringe. If I was going to make a play, it would have to before he stuck that thing in me. Brewer was all of ten feet away, with the gun. The woman was watching now, and I wondered what made a female like that tick. In any case, she could be discounted as no more than a bystander.

The chief inquisitor was ready now, and giving a little nod of satisfaction as he ejected two quick squirts from the syringe.

"I have to eliminate air bubbles," he explained conversationally. "It wouldn't do for you to die by accident. Well, I think we're about ready now."

I tensed in the chair. Any move I made was going to be a waste of time, but I preferred a nice clean bullet to that hellish needle. Once White-Suit got close to my arm, I would go for him, gun or no. But I wasn't dealing with a beginner.

"Relax, Preston," he advised, coming towards me. "You don't really imagine

I'm fool enough to stand where you can reach me? Forget it. This little beauty goes in at the back of your neck."

He walked around behind me, out of reach. The woman was getting excited, and I could see her breasts heaving up and down as she watched.

"In the belly, Preston. That's where the first one goes, if you move."

Tom Brewer had walked across and was now standing square in front of me, the automatic levelled at my middle. I couldn't see White-Suit, who was somewhere behind my chair, but I could see Brewer's eyes, and they were begging me to give him an excuse to squeeze that trigger. There wasn't a single damned thing I could do, and I gritted my teeth against the anticipated thrust of the needle. I felt the tip prick against the skin below my right ear.

A shot rang out.

I heard the syringe clatter to the ground. My senses were so sharpened that what followed was like watching a slow-motion movie. Brewer's head jerked up, so that he was staring over my shoulder. At the same time, his gun-hand began to move in an upward arc to meet this new threat. The syringe had fallen at my side. I scooped it up, and flung it, in one convulsive movement. It took him in the throat, and hung there, like some obscene insect. Then there was a second shot, and Brewer sank to his knees, blood coming from a ragged hole in his chest.

I was on my feet then, and swinging towards the entry. There stood Thompson, feet apart and ready to shoot anything that moved. White-Suit was kneeling on the ground, a great red patch spreading out across his shoulder. The woman leaped to her feet, and flung herself towards the automatic, where Brewer had dropped it on the paving. There wasn't time for niceties. She had her hand on the butt when I kicked her in the shoulder, sending her sprawling and swearing away. Then I put my hand inside Brewer's coat and pulled out the big revolver. My hand was shaking.

"You have some funny friends, Preston," greeted Thompson.

I nodded weakly. The situation was too recent for me to feel like repartee.

"I was never so pleased to see anybody in my entire life," I assured him. "How did you get here?"

"I saw the Caddy," he explained mysteriously.

"I don't follow that. What about the car?"

"I recognised it," he continued patiently. "Noticed it last time I was here. Beautiful car. So, when I saw it arrive at that place, I knew it couldn't be a coincidence. All I had to do was watch it come out. Once it came in this direction, the rest was easy.

"Wait a minute," I begged, "how do you mean, 'last time you were here'? When was that?"

"Yesterday," he explained. "I told you. This guy here, the one doing the mad doctor act, he's Arnold Hall."

I'd have got there quicker, if I hadn't

been in such a state of nervous tension. Now, I looked across at where the woman sat, rubbing at her kicked shoulder. The floppy hat and the glasses had come off in the activity. I went over to her, and said.

"My name is Preston. I don't believe we've met, Mrs Hadley."

Epilogue

I SAT behind my desk, while Thompson was sprawled all over a chair on the other side. The bottle of scotch was nearly at its end, but there was another in reserve. It had been an hour since we staggered in from police headquarters, and we had a lot of relaxing to catch up on.

"Oughta get a medal," decided my guest mysteriously.

"Who did?"

He waved a negligent hand.

"You — me — somebody. People like us, stopping all these wars, we oughta get something."

I nodded in friendly agreement. Then I shook my head.

"The only thing we were liable to get was two to five in the State penitentiary, if Brewer hadn't been such a canary."

He pursed his lips owlishly, then chuckled.

"He has a lovely voice, that Brewer."

Wounded as he was, Brewer had clutched desperately at the syringe which had lodged in his throat. His awkward movements had partially depressed the plunger, releasing some of the fluid into his system. Five minutes later, he was not merely willing to talk, it was almost impossible to stop him. He told us the whole story, over and over. He told it again to the police, when they arrived, and then to the medics, in their turn.

Gil Randall of Homicide had been the first on the scene, and it must have looked like a battlefield. Arnold Hall, was sitting against a wall, clutching his ruined shoulder, and was almost unconscious. We'd kept Brewer as upright as we could, in a chair with plenty of cushions. I had some vague recollection that he ought not to be prone until that wound had had professional attention. The drug, whatever it was, seemed to act as a pain-killer as well as a tongue-loosener, so he just sat there babbling away. Joyce Hadley had made two attempts to get at him, with murder clearly in mind, so we'd been compelled to tie her up.

Brewer confirmed everything I suspected, and added refinements I hadn't yet arrived at. Larry Palmer had picked the wrong man when he confided his ideas to Dexter Hadley. Hadley was already involved with Hall and the so-called export business, and he knew exactly where the markets were for the souped-up AG4B. Hadley thought it would be a simple matter to pay off Palmer, but he didn't know the nature of Arnold Hall. He also didn't know that Hall and his own wife had an intense thing going on the side. Joyce was a very ambitious lady, and she had no intention of wasting herself indefinitely on a man like Hadley. All the same, she wasn't the killer Pete Kowalski had made her out to be. On the night Palmer died, Hall had used her as a decoy. Palmer would never suspect anything wrong if Hadley's wife was involved. After a few drinks, Joyce had left, understanding that Brewer was going to persuade Palmer to sign away his rights. She hadn't even known the death was other than accidental until I came into the picture.

Her husband's murder was another matter. Hall had blamed him for the mishap with the switched earth-mover, and there was a lot of tension in the air. After he'd been to see me, Hadley had been drinking with Brewer, and confessed to him that he was concerned about Joyce's activities. Brewer reported to Hall, and Hall decided to eliminate Hadley, who was no longer really necessary to the project anyway. Brewer and Kowalski did the shooting, and Joyce was more relieved than upset. She was a very strange lady.

It was all too much for Randall to take in at one hearing, and we all trooped down to headquarters for endless hours of cross-examination and statements. I tossed up in my mind as to whether I'd admit to shooting Kowalski, but decided I might as well get the whole thing over in one hit. Randall looked at me oddly when I mentioned that part of it.

"Wondered whether you'd get around to that," he grunted.

"It was self-defence, Gil," I assured him. "The girl will speak for me."

"You'd better hope so. We got enough trouble in this town without every private dick shooting up the citizens like he was the Lone Ranger."

"He was going to kill the girl, godammit," I protested.

"So you say. Still, I have to admit, this other stuff'll go in your favour. You could just break even."

Break even. I thought back to his words, while Thompson was burbling on about medals.

"Somebody emptied this bottle," he announced accusingly.

I reached down for the refill and passed it over.

"Here," I said. "There's another case on the way over, courtesy of the Monkton City Globe. I'm their star reporter, did you know?"

"I didn't even know you could write," he advised me churlishly, wrenching ineffectually at the sealed bottle-top.

"Fat lot you know," I grumbled. "Inside man, that's me. I cover all the shootings, and the gunrunning. Stuff like that."

Thompson ignored that entirely.

"In the Westerns," he observed thoughtfully, "the hero always pulls these out with his teeth."

"Put it on the desk," I commanded. "Gotta study this. Work out a method. Gotta be methodical."

Dutifully, he leaned forward and set the offending bottle carefully between us. We both placed our fists on the desk, chins in the rest position and peered at the cap. A slender hand reached down and lifted the bottle away. We both looked up in protest. Mike Blair stood there, grinning down at us. Then, with one deft movement, she removed the cap. Thompson gave her a little handclap and I followed suit.

"Who's this lady? She smells nice," whispered Thompson, in a voice that probably didn't carry more than a block and a half.

"Colleague," I advised him. "Reporter colleague. Mike Blair, meet Sam Thompson, and Sam, you do the same."

Mike stared at him fondly.

"You're the man who saved this idiot's life today. I'm glad to know you, Sam."

"Lady, I would get up, but I can't seem to locate my feet," Thompson said. "Was it him I saved today? I save so many lives."

Mike made a little clicking noise with her tongue.

"I can see I'm not going to get far with you clowns this evening. Well, like the man said, if you can't beat 'em."

She dragged up a chair, produced a glass for herself, and poured out a measure.

"Mind if I join you?"

"Beautiful," said Sam.

A FOOT IN THE GRAVE
Bruce Marshall

About to be imprisoned and tortured in Buenos Aires, John Smith escapes, only to become involved in an aeroplane hijacking.

DEAD TROUBLE
Martin Carroll

Trespassing brought Jennifer Denning more than she bargained for. She was totally unprepared for the violence which was to lie in her path.

HOURS TO KILL
Ursula Curtiss

Margaret went to New Mexico to look after her sick sister's rented house and felt a sharp edge of fear when the absent landlady arrived.

THE DEATH OF ABBE DIDIER
Richard Grayson

Inspector Gautier of the Sûreté investigates three crimes which are strangely connected.

NIGHTMARE TIME
Hugh Pentecost

Have the missing major and his wife met with foul play somewhere in the Beaumont Hotel, or is their disappearance a carefully planned step in an act of treason?

BLOOD WILL OUT
Margaret Carr

Why was the manor house so oddly familiar to Elinor Howard? Who would have guessed that a Sunday School outing could lead to murder?

THE DRACULA MURDERS
Philip Daniels

The Horror Ball was interrupted by a spectral figure who warned the merrymakers they were tampering with the unknown.

THE LADIES
OF LAMBTON GREEN
Liza Shepherd

Why did murdered Robin Colquhoun's picture pose such a threat to the ladies of Lambton Green?

CARNABY
AND THE GAOLBREAKERS
Peter N. Walker

Detective Sergeant James Aloysius Carnaby-King is sent to prison as bait. When he joins in an escape he is thrown headfirst into a vicious murder hunt.

MUD IN HIS EYE
Gerald Hammond

The harbourmaster's body is found mangled beneath Major Smyle's yacht. What is the sinister significance of the illicit oysters?

THE SCAVENGERS
Bill Knox

Among the masses of struggling fish in the *Tecta*'s nets was a larger, darker, ominously motionless form . . . the body of a skin diver.

DEATH IN ARCADY
Stella Phillips

Detective Inspector Matthew Furnival works unofficially with the local police when a brutal murder takes place in a caravan camp.

STORM CENTRE
Douglas Clark

Detective Chief Superintendent Masters, temporarily lecturing in a police staff college, finds there's more to the job than a few weeks relaxation in a rural setting.

THE MANUSCRIPT MURDERS
Roy Harley Lewis

Antiquarian bookseller Matthew Coll, acquires a rare 16th century manuscript. But when the Dutch professor who had discovered the journal is murdered, Coll begins to doubt its authenticity.

SHARENDEL
Margaret Carr

Ruth didn't want all that money. And she didn't want Aunt Cass to die. But at Sharendel things looked different. She began to wonder if she had a split personality.

MURDER TO BURN
Laurie Mantell

Sergeants Steven Arrow and Lance Brendon, of the New Zealand police force, come upon a woman's body in the water. When the dead woman is identified they begin to realise that they are investigating a complex fraud.

YOU CAN HELP ME
Maisie Birmingham

Whilst running the Citizens' Advice Bureau, Kate Weatherley is attacked with no apparent motive. Then the body of one of her clients is found in her room.

DAGGERS DRAWN
Margaret Carr

Stacey Manston was the kind of girl who could take most things in her stride, but three murders were something different . . .